D1501004

Masters of Interior Space

A Novel about the Spiritual Life

Lawrence Tucker, SOLT

En Route Books and Media, LLC
Saint Louis, Missouri

En Route Books and Media, LLC

5705 Rhodes Avenue

St. Louis, MO 63109

Contact us at **contact@enroutebooksandmedia.com**

Front Cover Credit: Danielle C. Mesa

Back Cover and Interior Image Credit: Emiliano Gil

Copyright 2023 Lawrence Tucker, SOLT

ISBN-13: 979-8-88870-029-7

Library of Congress Control Number:

Available at https://catalog.loc.gov/

All rights reserved. No part of this book may be reproduced, stored in a retrieval system, or transmitted in any form, or by any means, electronic, mechanical, photocopying, or otherwise, without the prior written permission of the author.

DEDICATION

This book is dedicated to the happy memory of
Fr. Joseph C. Henchey, CSS, STD

(6/2/1930 - 4/7/2021)

a teacher, and a true
Master of Interior Space

TABLE OF CONTENTS

CHAPTER ONE

"I wouldn't go in there, Scoot!" I cried out. But it was too late. Scooter had already entered the foreboding, dark chamber that displayed a sign which read:

Authorized personnel only; all others... <u>STAY OUT!</u>

The last thing I heard Scooter shout just before the heavy iron door, as if it had a mind of its own, slammed shut behind him, was:

"Don't worry, Doc; I'm pretty sure I'm authorized!"

I guess I'll have to be the one to tell this story because I really doubt Scooter will ever get around to it. Scooter's real name is Stuart McKenzie, but everyone just calls him Scooter because ever since he was a kid he always seemed to be up to some sort of adventure. So the nickname, "Scooter," or simply, "Scoot"— just seemed to fit.

My name is James Laughton, and I'm a history professor at the University of Notre Dame. Scooter was one of my best students. It wasn't that he was brilliant or endowed with an exceptionally high IQ. No... his gift was his heart. He had a deep and a sincere love for humanity and the story of human-kind. His enthusiasm in class was infectious, and his mere presence elevated the entire lesson in a truly marvelous way. He received his B. A. Degree in History... *cum laude.*

Stuart had a profound love for God and for the poor, along with an exceptionally well-developed prayer life. This, more than anything else, is what animated his caring attitude toward the human family. And so it was only natural that, with this kind of winning disposition, Scooter had many friends both on as well as off campus. I was one of his many friends.

At the time the events I'm about to recount took place, Stuart was a 21-year-old young adult. He was a good looking fellow, but not so striking as to attract Hollywood scouts or modeling agents. At 5'11", 170lbs, wavy black hair, brown eyes, and a medium build, his appearance tended to blend in rather than stand out.

The thing that really distinguished Stuart was his spirit. If someone chose to sit with him in the cafeteria, within five minutes they would sense they were in the presence of a special person; that this was someone they were comfortable with and would like to be friends with.

While I would not describe Stuart as being charismatic in the "loud" sense, he was definitely charismatic in the quiet, mysterious sense. He radiated something intangible, but nonetheless real and unmistakable.

I, on the other hand, am not blessed with that... *je ne sais quoi*... which Scoot had in such abundance. Suffice to say that

I could serve as the poster child for the typical, fuddy-duddy, bespectacled college professor... complete with a full white beard and scraggly white hair. I am friendly and conversant, but something of a dreamer. Most people would say I came across as someone who is more or less lost in thought... almost all the time.

I live off campus in the family home, which I inherited. It's a big old, three-story, five-bedroom farm house that sits on one hundred beautiful acres of gentle, rolling hills, just outside the city limits of South Bend, Indiana. At the time, I was 55 years old. But with white hair, glasses, my customary, old-fashioned Harris Tweed blazer and vintage, Dunhill English tobacco pipe, my appearance was more like that of a 75-year-old retired English gentleman merrily enroute to his serene country estate.

When I was 42 years old, I married a 38-year-old English professor named Cheryl Morgan. I believe the marriage would have worked out beautifully had Cheryl not died suddenly from a pulmonary aneurysm upon our return to the USA after our honeymoon in London. I never remarried.

Nevertheless, I was at peace and lived my life like a man with a purpose. I became a student of history because I believed the human story was more than just the recording of dates and events. For me, it is a relational phenomenon; the story of the loving relationship between God and humanity... between a Father and his children.

Knowing my area of specialization was the *Spanish Golden Age*, which began in 1492, one can imagine how completely thrilled and excited I was when I received a call from the Prefect of the Vatican's... *Congregation for the Causes of Saints...* asking me if I would conduct a portion of the research needed in preparation for the possible beatification of the Servant of God, Queen Isabella I of Castile (Spain).

The Prefect said he would like me to go to Spain... Granada, in particular... for a week or so in June to review certain historical documents. Stuart had just graduated from Notre Dame with a B.A. in History, and following the summer break he was planning to return to the campus to begin work on an M.A. in History. So I invited him to accompany me as a research assistant; all expenses paid, plus a reasonable stipend. He jumped at the opportunity.

To keep everything within a tight budget, we decided to take a train to New York City. And from there... thanks to a good friend in Spain, Alvaro Mendoza... we would board an old tramp steamer named the *Rocinante* (Don Quixote's horse) to Spain. The *Rocinante* was very similar to the tramp that was featured in *Jurassic Park...* the *SS Venture*.

Raul, the captain of the *Rocinante*, was Alvaro's brother and a good Catholic. It all worked out well and things were going along as planned until that fateful day when we were preparing to leave the ancient port city of Málaga, Spain (birthplace of Pablo Picasso) for the USA, with one stop in Algiers, Algeria.

While in Spain, one of the things I was personally interested in trying to discover was a legendary, four-foot-tall, carved wooden statue of Queen Isabella, which was said to represent the most accurate rendition of the queen's appearance; especially with regard to her countenance.

The statue was reputed to be fabricated in such a way that it could be hung upon a wall; a style very popular at the time. It was also said to be associated with a similar statue of King Ferdinand; the two statues formed one glorious display of the Catholic Monarchs. However, the statue of the King, unlike that of the Queen, was not reported to be a particularly pleasing likeness of his majesty.

But what was even more fascinating was that the statue of the queen was said to be such a perfect likeness of her that if you spoke to it you could have the impression she was alive and listening to your every word. Some people even reported having actually experienced her speaking to them.

I would never mention this to anyone, but I was secretly hoping there was a grain of truth to this enchanting legend. I used to imagine the various questions I would ask regarding decisions made during her reign, as well as inquiries into her intense spiritual life. If the legend was true, so many unanswered questions that historians have concerning the *Spanish Golden Age* could be answered... by the Queen herself!

Of course, being a serious historian, this sort of thinking was simply a playful, relaxing excursion into a fantasy that, no doubt, has been the recurring daydream of every historian who ever lived.

Most historians give no credence to the stories of "the living statue," and write it off as just another legend... in an age replete with legends. The very notion of acquiring historical data from a talking statue is the sort of hilarity that enlivens a university faculty dinner party after all present have ingested a bit too much wine.

But I have often asked myself this question: from whence comes the historical and archaeological information we do manage to discover? How is it we find that which we find? Considering the plethora of artifacts and ancient documents out there that we could perhaps discover; how is it we discover the specific ones that we *do* discover? At times, it seems as though they were selected and we were led to them by some mysterious, beneficent force.

How were the *Qumran Scrolls* discovered? This was a monumental discovery... and how did it come about? A humble, Bedouin shepherd happened upon them stashed away in a cave in a remote, desert area near the Dead Sea. While we don't always find what we are looking for, it seems that we *do* find what we *really* need... exactly when we need it! Could this phenomenon be the expression of some sort of Divine Providence? I must admit... the secularized atmosphere of present day academia notwithstanding... I'm inclined to think it is.

And so the mysterious possibility of somehow gleaning historical information from a five-hundred-year-old carved wooden statue does not strike me as being quite as ludicrous as it might initially appear to be. I guess you could say that when it comes to doing historical research, I approach it with a professionally-trained, but open mind.

The Spanish people had a name for the queen's statue. They called it: *La Imagen Viva* (The Living Image). The belief is that it was carved around the time of the Reconquista (1492). The last somewhat credible reference we have of its existence is from the year 1588, immediately following the British defeat of the Spanish Armada.

Some believe that if it did exist, Miguel de Cervantes, who was a Third Order Franciscan and author of what is considered by many to be the greatest novel ever written... *Don Quixote,* appreciating its artistic, religious, and historical value, would have taken charge of it and hid it away somewhere safe to protect it from those who might be tempted to misuse or destroy it.

Strangely enough, the fate of *La Imagen Viva*... that is, its disappearance from the historical record... was also the fate of the mortal remains of Cervantes. He was interred, as he requested, in the *Convent of the Barefoot Trinitarians* in Madrid. But when the Convent was being restored in 1673, his remains went missing and were not discovered until 2015 by forensic anthropologist Francisco Etxeberria.

Stuart and I searched and searched for *La Imagen Viva*, following one lead after another, but we could not locate it. At times, we both had this strange feeling we were getting close...

very close! We felt confident it did exist and that we would certainly find it. But eventually, due to the Vatican research project I was responsible for, regrettably, but understandably... we had to give up the search.

Far from being the end of the story, however, this is where the *real* story begins. Since I, James Laughton, have been selected by providence to tell this wondrous story, a unique story that does not fit so neatly into any particular category, I feel compelled to prepare you, the reader, with the following quote by the English historian, Christopher Dawson:

"American literature has never been content to be just one among the many literatures of the Western World. It has always aspired to be the literature of not only a new continent, but of a new world."

CHAPTER TWO

It all began when we boarded the tramp steamer, *Rocinante*, for the return voyage to New York City, with one overnight stop across the Mediterranean Sea in the North African coastal city of Algiers, Algeria.

As the ship pulled away from the beautiful Spanish port, Stuart and I took a stroll around the deck to enjoy the sunset and the cool, evening air. We reflected on how, while we didn't find the artifact we were hoping to find, we did successfully complete the Vatican-sponsored research project.

Stuart's Spanish was much better than my own, and at one point in our stroll, as we passed 3 sailors who were huddled together and conversing in a hushed tone, Scoot gently pulled me aside up against the outer railing of the ship, and in an excited whisper said:

"Doc... did you catch what those sailors were talking about?"

"No, Stuart, I could barely hear them; I didn't catch any of it."

"Doc... you're not going to believe this! They were discussing *La Imagen Viva*! They were wondering why it was aboard the ship and where it could possibly be going. One asked whether it would be safe in the secret, special storage room deep in the hold of the ship where it had been stowed. Doc, can this possibly be true? That the very thing we have been searching for has been right under our feet this whole time?"

"When it comes to this particular artifact, Stuart," I replied, "I would say that just about *anything* is possible! Come on… let's find our way down to the hold of the ship and see what we can discover. The fact that somehow we were in the right place at just the right time to be privy to such a pertinent conversation causes me to think we are being led. Therefore, I suggest we follow this lead and try to find the secret storage room the sailors spoke of."

We proceeded to descend into the bowels of the old cargo ship, moving from one level to the next, until we arrived at what appeared to be the very bottom of the vessel. Slowly, using the greatest amount of stealth we could muster, Scoot and I began to traverse the eerie, poorly lit corridors of the ship's hold searching for something that would have the appearance of a special room designated for the storage of exceptionally valuable cargo. We were imagining something akin to a large, walk-in vault.

As we made our way through those damp, dark, musty spaces, we passed numerous signs warning that passengers were not permitted on that level. Nevertheless, we continued to push on, animated by the great excitement instilled in us by the new information mysteriously provided by some unsuspecting sailors… just when we had given up all hope of ever finding *La Imagen Viva*.

Quietly, as we moved deeper and deeper into the fetid hold of the ship, so as not to draw any attention to our presence, we communicated with one another using our eyes, hands, and facial expressions. At one point, I sensed that Stuart was no longer close behind me. I turned and saw that he had come to a halt around ten yards back.

As I approached him, I could see he was staring into a shadowy niche in the corridor wall that was about the size of the entrance to a normal flat in London; except that it was murky and dark and impossible to tell what, if anything, was there. We looked at one another and Stuart, pointing into the shadows, in a soft but clear whisper, said:

"It's in there; the special storage room is right here; I know it... I can feel it. It's here... I'm certain."

"But Scoot," I said, "there's *nothing* there. It's just a scary, dark, empty space; probably filled with mold, cobwebs, and who knows what else!"

"Exactly, Doc; the perfect place to hide a treasure vault! I'm going in."

Before I could stop him, Scooter had stepped directly into the shadows and disappeared from sight. Suddenly, however, to my great relief, a small light switched on... probably a unit activated by motion... and was shining on a sign posted over a huge, heavy metal door; a door much sturdier looking than any we had passed thus far. The sign read:

Authorized Personnel only; all others... <u>STAY OUT!</u>

In the event there was some sort of hazard or security measure that would be activated upon the unauthorized opening of the chamber door, I did not want Stuart to be the first to enter, so I moved in front of him and clasped the large door handle with both hands and gave it a good pull, but it would not open; it was locked. I turned to tell Scoot it was locked, but as I turned, he had already slipped past me, grabbed the handle, pulled... and the vault door opened!

I yelled to him frantically not to go in... but it was too late. Without any hesitation, he had already entered the foreboding, pitch black, interior chamber of the vault; and the massive door immediately slammed shut behind him. I quickly tried to open the door, but once again... for me at least... it was locked.

Feeling utterly helpless, I stood there in front of the door— motionless and in shock. Quickly coming to my senses, however, I realized that my standing there meant the light would remain illuminated for any passing sailor to see, so I stepped back into the narrow corridor.

I no sooner positioned myself in the corridor, facing the dark niche with my back to the wall, when out of nowhere and without any sound or warning, a young female sailor I did not recognize came strolling in front of me and, with a french accent, said:

"Well, monsieur... don't *you* look like someone who is about to receive an important mission!"

How strange her words sounded to me. I was so baffled and confused by them that when I looked up to see where this mysterious sailor had gone, she was nowhere to be found. Adding to my perplexity was the fact that she said nothing at all about my presence in a part of the ship that was completely off limits to passengers.

Suddenly the chamber door opened and closed with a grinding, metal-on-metal noise. Then the light switched on, and quickly off. And finally, as if he were an apparition coming forth from an ancient tomb… Stuart was standing in front of me with an expression of astonishment on his face I will never forget. Just when I thought things could not get more incomprehensible, the tale that Scoot began to relate regarding his experience while in the vault… a period of no more than two minutes… was so wondrous and bewildering that, on the spot, I gave up all hope of ever experiencing again what is generally referred to as a "normal" state of mind.

CHAPTER THREE

"Are you OK, Stuart? Is the statue there? Did you see it?" I asked.

"Did I *see* it? Doc... it SPOKE to me!" replied Stuart, with great excitement. "I had a *lengthy* conversation with it!"

"But Scoot, you were only in there for no more than two minutes; what are you talking about? Tell me, Scooter... calm down; take your time and tell me everything that happened."

"When the door opened," Stuart began, "I quickly entered; but not completely under my own power; it was as though I was being pulled, or drawn in by someone other than myself. Which is why I yelled to you not to worry because the sensation caused me to feel that, somehow, I was in fact "authorized."

When the vault door slammed shut behind me, I felt around in the darkness to see if I could locate a light switch, but I could not find one. As I peered into the pitch black, I noticed something beginning to glow about ten feet away from where I was standing. It was radiating a bluish light, and as I started to move toward it, the light became brighter and I was able to discern the hues of many other colors as well.

Then I heard someone call my name... *'Stuart... Stuart, dear; come closer. Do not be afraid'*. At first, I thought perhaps

15

it was you calling to me from the other side of the chamber door. But I quickly realized, as strange as it seemed, that it was a woman's voice and it was coming from the colorful, radiant object I was cautiously approaching.

When I was within three feet of this mysterious, luminescent object, I realized that, beyond the shadow of a doubt, it was… *La Imagen Viva*! She was approximately four feet tall and positioned directly above the wood shipping crate she would normally have been in. As she hovered in place, she was gently moving her hands, motioning to me to come closer.

She had a wonderful, warm, radiant smile… like Glinda, the Good Witch of the North in The Wizard of Oz. In fact, I believe her smile was the source of all the resplendent light. But more astounding still was the fact that she was speaking! And not just that she was speaking, but that she was speaking… *to me!* Queen Isabella herself, Doc; it was marvelous!"

"Are you sure it was Queen Isabella, Stuart?" I asked.

"Oh, without question, Doc; she identified herself by name." responded Scoot.

"Exactly *how* did she do that, Scoot?" I enquired.

"It was the first thing she said when I was finally close enough to make eye contact with her," replied Scooter. "She said:

'Fear not, Stuart; be at peace. I am Queen Isabella of Castile, and I have a message for you from your poor little brother… Jesus.'"

"A message from GOD!" I blurted out in total amazement, "What was the message?"

"She said that I had been chosen to fulfill a mission she had been given, but unfortunately... never completed," replied Stuart.

"Stuart, with regard to this 'mission,' can you remember her exact words?" I asked, in a serious tone.

"Yes, I do remember what she said; maybe not verbatim, but yes, I definitely recall the essence of her statement; how could I ever forget it! It isn't everyday one has a vibrant conversation with a monarch from the sixteenth century!" replied Scooter, with a sparkle in his eyes. "She said:

"The Lord gave me an important mission, but I misunderstood it; the same way that St. Francis of Assisi misunderstood the words spoken to him by Jesus from the cross in the church of San Damiano. Jesus' words to Francis were... 'Rebuild my church.' The church of San Damiano was abandoned and in terrible disrepair, so of course Francis thought the Lord was asking him to rebuild it; which he immediately set about doing.

But actually, since the Catholic Church had run aground spiritually and was in a very sad state, the Lord was calling Francis to renew and 'rebuild' the entire, universal Catholic Church... at the spiritual level.

Similarly, the night before I met with Christopher Columbus in Santa Fe, Granada, to sign the Capitulations which would facilitate what would come to be known as perhaps the most consequential exploratory sea voyage in human history, I had a dream.

In this powerful dream, Jesus appeared before me and said: 'Come... live in me; you will discover a new world!'

"*Naturally, the next day when the explorer, Columbus, went on and on about how he would discover a new world, I believed that the Lord was guiding me and had prepared me the night before to give my approval. Therefore, filled with spiritual confidence, I did not hesitate to sponsor the expedition.*

But on November 26th, 1504, when at last I arrived in heaven, I was shown how that was not the mission the Lord was referring to in my dream. The mission he was in fact inviting me to was an interior one; one in which I would discover the wonders of an even deeper, gifted interior life with God. But, being all too human, like Francis... I misconstrued the message.

Nevertheless, the Lord worked with my good will, as well as my human limitations, and the Christian Faith was brought to places it had never been before; to people Europeans did not even know existed. As for the original mission— the Lord decided to wait for the right time and the right person to come along. This is the right time, and you, Stuart, are that 'right person'."

"But I don't understand, Stuart. What was it the Queen was being invited to do, but did *not* manage to do?" I interjected.

"Good question, Doc. She said that it wasn't a case of her never having had an interior life, but that the Lord was inviting her into an even deeper experience of personal, spiritual communion with the three divine persons. On the eve of that momentous decision to sponsor Columbus' voyage, the Lord was offering her a new outpouring of divine love and wisdom so she could assess the proposed journey with greater insight and prudence.

This wisdom from above would have enabled her to handle the capitulations... the legal contract made with Columbus... with greater wisdom and spiritual sensitivity; the Lord knows the hearts of men much better than anyone ever could.

Also, having just defeated the Moors in their last stronghold at Granada, the Queen had finally solidified the Catholic identity of Spain. This being the case, the Lord was offering the Queen the opportunity to be an even *more* luminous Catholic leader than she already was."

CHAPTER FOUR

Stuart continued with his report and said the Queen went on to describe in greater depth the historical context within which her original mission was situated. She told him that the good Lord knew the world was on the cusp of an unprecedented period, which is often referred to as the *"Age of Discovery."* But in actuality, from an ethical perspective at least, it turned out to be more an age of greed, grasping and vicious, cutthroat competition.

The hope, therefore, was that Spain, having the moral high ground and being the first country "on site," would be in the perfect position to set the tone for a humbler, more respectful response to the *encounter with…* as opposed to *discovery of…* all those new peoples and lands.

But even more to the point, the Queen, being able to discern all her options with greater wisdom and insight, would have had the interior freedom to simply decide against the proposed voyage altogether; and instead, focus on the internal development of the newly constituted Spanish nation itself.

After all, although the Spanish Empire, which began in 1492 (the end of the reconquista) and lasted nearly five centuries, brought considerable wealth, power, and prestige to Spain, it did not bring lasting peace and security.

Furthermore, all of her subsidiary colonies are now independent nations and are no longer ruled by Spain. In addition, as evidenced by the horrendous Spanish Civil War of 1936-39 that left one million dead and the nation in such a dysfunctional and fragmented condition that it ended up being governed by a dictatorship for the next 35 years, authentic, wholistic, *integral* development, the Grand Prize that all nations strive for, continued to elude Spain.

And so it would seem that, as Shakespere said so well, all the fuss about the Empire was, in the final analysis... *"much ado about nothing."* Talk about spinning one's wheels and getting nowhere, human beings seem to have a certain proclivity for setting up their own version of the hamster's running wheel whenever an opportunity to actually move forward in an integrated way presents itself.

And I would not be at all surprised if this indicates that, absent a firm belief in divine providence, humans prefer to live in the imaginary security of a "cage."

I was amazed at the amount of information the Queen had shared with Stuart in such a short period of time, but according to Scoot... this was just the tip of the iceberg! I suggested we move to a more secure place and continue the conversation in the privacy of our cabin.

After having ascended a number of levels, we arrived at the main deck where we took a couple of minutes to breathe the fresh, evening, Mediterranean Sea air in an attempt to purge ourselves of the putrid fumes we had been inhaling down in the ship's hold. Once we were "comfortably" seated in our modestly furnished quarters, Scoot on a hard wooden chair with an old life preserver serving as a seat cushion, and me on the edge of my rickety, fold-up bunk... Stuart began:

"Doc, I suppose all of this is probably overwhelming for you; I know it is for me. But what I have shared with you so far is just the smallest part of the whole conversation. You could call it the... *Introduction*."

"You mean there's *more*, Scoot?" I replied with astonishment.

"MUCH more, Doc. I haven't even gotten to the mission yet. Hang in there; the more bewildering it gets, the more it starts to actually make sense. I don't know how that works, but it does.

"The Queen said the Columbus expedition fed right into man's inherent weakness; the propensity to seek his purpose and fulfillment in the world around him... instead of looking within; which for human beings, is the only place it will ever be found. St. Augustine, in *The City of God*, pointed out the folly of man's attempts to set up a utopian kingdom in this world. And, in contrast, how Jesus taught us that... *The kingdom of God is within you* (Luke 17:21).

"The colonialism that ensued on the heels of that momentous voyage was nothing less than an ethnocentric feeding frenzy among European nations competing for global expansion and dominance. Once again, man's attention had become focused on that which is external and less meaningful; as compared to the sublime mystery of his own, gifted, inner life with God.

"The spirit of faith and prayer that was so characteristic of Christendom and the medieval period was about to give way to the banality and worldliness of the modern period. A new and enticing door had been opened, and it was as though, rushing recklessly through that door, all of Christian Europe had lost its moral composure and state of interior recollection."

"I am speechless, Stuart." I said, "This is beyond amazing; it's breathtaking! To listen to you recount Queen Isabella's observations regarding the Age of Discovery, as well as her insightful historical and spiritual analysis of that same period, is just, well… I feel as though I'm dreaming! Her central point reminds me of something one of my favorite historians, Christopher Dawson, said:

'The modern dilemma is essentially a spiritual one; and every one of its aspects— moral, political, and scientific— brings us back to the need for a religious solution.'

"Yes, Doc," chimed in Stuart excitedly… signaling total affirmation for his professor's astute observation, "and that brings us to the Queen's final point… the 'mission.' I'm sure I can remember this critical, particularly impressive part well enough to give an accurate paraphrase of her words."

Here in the next chapter is what she shared.

CHAPTER FIVE

"*Stuart, the Lord has chosen you for a special work. He would like you to be a light of hope in the darkness of this world. Not light such as I am radiating right now, which is perceived by the senses, but a type of spiritual light that can only be perceived by the soul. The world, once again, is at an historic turning point and all indications are that, as has happened in the past, it is about to completely lose its moral compass and spiritual equilibrium.*

"*As though it were a sequel to the misbegotten Age of Discovery, the people and nations of this era are seeking the solutions to all their problems, and the answers to all their questions, in the external world around them. They're rambling on about the real possibility of discovering a 'new world' somewhere in outer space.*

"*What has been lost in this hysteria, Scooter, is the proper understanding of 'Man.' Man has never been, is not now, and never will be the master of the universe. That's not who he is; that's who God is. Complete mastery and dominance over the world is not man's gift or his vocation. Man's true gift is an interior one; his unlimited capacity for love and communion with God.*

"Therefore, for the sake of simplicity, we could say that hu-man beings are called to be... 'masters of <u>interior</u> space.' This is how we have been created; the interior life is our gift area. With regard to the world, human beings are called to be, to the best of their ability, stewards of our Father's creation.

"Hopefully, Scooter, after this explanation, you are begin-ning to understand the importance of your assignment. At a dangerous and precarious time in world history, when people are regressing and falling into the age-old error of imagining that all their problems will be solved if they can just discover a new world 'out there', you and your team, Scooter, will witness to the truth that if they pursue the interior life, they will indeed discover a 'new world;' the one they were created to discover, and the one that will satisfy the deepest longings and the most ardent desires of the human heart and soul.

"If you accept this vocation, Scooter, you will need two things; you will need a team, and you and your team will need a spiritual 'tune-up' regarding prayer and the ways of the Spirit. Your team has already been hand picked; and with your special mission in mind, your formator has also been carefully selected."

"But, excuse me for interrupting, Your Highness, but..."

"Stuart... there is no need to be so formal. Now that I am in Heaven, you may address me as... Isabella. Or, if you like, feel free to simply call me... Bella."

"Oh, yes, of course, Your Bellaness… I mean, BELLA! OK, great! That's a lot easier. I guess being in Heaven has its advantages."

"It certainly does, Stuart."

"Oh, and while we're on the subject, you can call me Scooter… or just, Scoot; that's what all my friends call me."

"Thank you, Scooter; what a delightful nickname."

"Well, Bella, what I was about to say is… I don't understand why I was chosen for this work. I'm a sinner and I don't have any special skills or talents. Also… I think I'm probably too young for any sort of 'special mission' assignment."

"Why God chooses who he does is a mystery known only to God. He knows the hearts of men, Scooter. Remember how, through the prophet Samuel, He chose David — a humble young man serving in the fields as a shepherd. For this particular work, your status as a young person is precisely what is called for; your youthful energy and enthusiasm will be invaluable to the mission.

"Also, the fact that you are a layman is significant. What is needed right now is a powerful witness by the lay faithful of the beauty and importance of the interior life for the human person; whose dignity is being trampled upon more severely with each passing day.

"This much I do know, however; the Lord is very pleased with your virtuous life, and your love for, and consequent development in, prayer. He recognizes that you have already entered into the quiet prayer of the heart. This indicates that you now

have the capacity to listen closely to the Lord as he guides and forms you from within. Therefore, Scooter, based on this fact alone, you are indeed ready for a special assignment.

"Now that you have had the work explained to you, I have to ask you, Stuart, will you accept this invitation to serve?"

"Yes, Bella, I do accept this special mission; although I still feel most unsuited and unworthy of such a privileged calling."

"Perfect, Stuart! This humility is perhaps the main reason you have been chosen. By the grace of God you have given your assent and so it is now time to move on. As of this moment, you will be granted a new effusion of the Holy Spirit. You will be supplied with wonderful gifts that will help you to succeed in your service to our Father's loving plan. You will do amazing things; all of them rooted in love. As Jesus said... when comparing his works to those of his followers... 'They will do even greater things!'

"But I must warn you, Scooter... there will be obstacles. The enemies of God will be searching for you and they will do everything in their power to thwart, and/or destroy... The Masters of Interior Space. Be forewarned , therefore, and be on the alert. You will not be alone, however. God has seen fit to give you two heavenly assistants: Thérèse of Lisieux and Charles de Foucauld. They will accompany you spiritually on your journey. And, when you most need them, they will be there to assist you."

"Wow, that's a relief, Bella! But I'm curious; of all the possible candidates, why were those two chosen?" inquired Stuart.

"Good question, Stuart. Let me explain. Yves Congar, the great Dominican theologian whom many would argue was the single most formative influence on Vatican Council II, stated that:

'The mystical beacons that the hand of God has set aflame on the threshold of the atomic century are called... Thérèse of Lisieux and Charles de Foucauld.'

"Both these saints were contemplative missionaries; Thérèse in the Carmel at Lisieux, and Charles in the Sahara Desert. Thérèse was born when Charles was fifteen years old, and she died when he was thirty nine years old. They were contemporaries but there is no indication that they knew one another. Nevertheless, they were both moved by the Spirit in a similar, powerful direction.

"They witnessed to the Gospel not through preaching but by way of a sacrificial life filled with love. Due to the crisis of Truth, which has been a blight upon the present age, words no longer have the power they once had. The only language that has credibility anymore is the language of life; the example of a life lived in the Spirit speaks volumes! This is the gift that Thérèse and Charles gave to the modern world. And this is why they were chosen to accompany you; your mission is very similar to theirs, except that The Masters will be on the move, rather than fixed in one place."

"This is all starting to sound kind of neat, Bella. And I like the name... Masters of Interior Space." responded Scooter.

"The only reason for the name, Scooter, is to keep before you the nobility, dignity, and high spiritual calling of Man, and the reality that human beings are created for truly great and beautiful things; not the vapid, mundane, uninspired nonsense of the worldly minded. Now, let's move on to some of the more pertinent details."

"Wait, please... hold on a second, Bella. I think I understand what you're saying, but what I don't understand is... what is it I'm actually supposed to do?"

"Nothing!" responded the Queen.

"Now I'm completely confused!" said Scoot, "You mean my mission is to do... nothing?"

"Nothing... and Everything!" explained the Queen.

"Please, Bella, stop playing with me! I need to know what I should do."

"In Holy Scripture, Stuart, we read about a man who approached Jesus and asked what work he should do to be saved; and Jesus simply told him he should believe in the one God has sent. Jesus also told us that without him, we can do... NOTHING! But with him, we can do... EVERYTHING! You are living and moving in the Spirit now, Scooter, so Jesus will be at work in you; he will be doing all the heavy lifting! Be at peace my son; in time, you will understand."

CHAPTER SIX

"When your ship docks in Algiers, disembark and go directly to the Cathedral of The Sacred Heart. This is where your team will meet together for the first time. Your team will consist of four members: you, the leader; Dr. Laughton, who will serve as your counselor and as the 'scribe' of the mission. He will document everything and eventually compile it into book form.

"Charlotte Mahfoudh, a Berber from Tamanrasset, Algeria, and Tobias Trisong, a Tibetan from the Seychelles, both of whom you shall meet shortly, will round out your team of four. Dr. Laughton has already been prepped by Thérèse, the Little Flower. Just now she walked past him in the corridor disguised as a sailor, and said:

"'Well, monsieur... don't you look like someone who is about to receive an important mission!'"

"Yes, Stuart," I interjected excitedly, "that's exactly what happened! Of course, I could never have guessed who it was, although she did have a french accent. But please continue, Stuart... sorry to interrupt your train of thought. Bella was describing the team; what else did she have to say?"

"Well, Doc," replied Scoot, "she did have more to say, but this part is pretty much the final section of that conversation.

I asked her how I would be able to find Charlotte and Tobias at the Cathedral, and she said:

"Don't worry... they will find you! Both have already been briefed by the Spirit regarding the mission, and Charlotte knows what you look like and what you will be wearing. When all of you meet up at the Cathedral, Charlotte will explain the next step in the journey. My role in this mission, Stuart, is now complete. I will leave you in the competent hands of my friends, Thérèse and Charles. In Heaven, Scooter, everyone is a saint, so we are all on a first name basis. I will of course be praying for you, and that, you can be sure of! Adios, Scooter. I enjoyed our conversation."

"Stuart... do you realize that it took almost half an hour for you to recount for me your conversation with the Queen, but you were only in the chamber for about two minutes!" I said. "Clearly, something supernatural took place in there. It would just be impossible for anyone to fabricate all that de-tailed material in 2 minutes. Because of this, I am indeed convinced that we have been given a special mission. Perhaps our Vatican assignment regarding the beatification of Queen Isabella was some sort of prelude, or stepping-stone, to this new mission."

"Oh, I don't think there's any question about that, Doc;" replied Stuart, "without the Vatican assignment, we would have never found *La Imagen Viva*."

"By the way, Stuart, did Bella ever say what she was doing in the hold of a rickety old tramp steamer on its way to New York City?"

"No, Doc; she never said anything about that, and I never brought it up. I guess she wants to remain in the 'witness protection program' she has been in for the past few hundred years."

"Yes, it certainly does seem that way, Stuart."

We arrived in Algiers at around 9am and went directly to the Cathedral, which was within walking distance of the port. The Cathedral is difficult to describe because of its unique architecture, but suffice to say, it is magnificent, beautiful, super creative, and very inspiring.

The Cathedral uses chairs rather than pews, so we entered, chose a couple of chairs in the back, and sat down. It was very calm with only a few people near the sanctuary praying quietly. We were seated for only about 30 seconds when a striking young woman wearing beautiful, traditional Berber garments came and sat next to Stuart.

"Hello, Stuart," she said in perfect English, "I am Charlotte. The Holy Spirit told me to look for a young man my age wearing a Notre Dame t-shirt."

"Hello, Charlotte," responded Stuart, a bit startled, "the Queen told me you would find us. This is Dr. Laughton... but you probably already knew that."

"I have been so looking forward to meeting both of you," said Charlotte with enthusiasm, "but please, call me Charlie; that's what everyone calls me here in Algeria. Most of the people I associate with know that my parents named me after St.

Charles de Foucauld. My great grandfather was a friend of Charles and was formed in the spiritual life by him.

"This desert spirituality has been passed on in my family through each generation, right up until my own. Let's step outside into the garden; I would like you to meet Tobias, who goes by the nickname Toby... he is waiting for us there."

"Hello... I'm Toby," said Tobias as he rose to his feet from the concrete bench he was sitting on, "Welcome to North Africa!"

Toby was 21 years old, five-foot-seven, 140lbs, with medium length straight black hair and a wonderful, outgoing personality. He was a student at the University of Seychelles (UniSey) and had just completed the first 4 years of a 6-year program for a Master's Degree in Peace and Conflict Resolution.

Toby's parents were Tibetans and were born in Lhasa, Tibet. His parents were practicing Buddhists. But not only were they Buddhists, they were actually related to Gyalwa Rinpoche... the 14th Dali Lama. When the Chinese invaded Tibet in 1959, the Dali Lama escaped to India. Many members of his extended family, such as Toby's family, also sought refuge in India.

Toby's parents were high school teachers and ended up settling in the Seychelles; which is where Toby was born. When Toby was eight years old, his parents were murdered by Somali pirates. Toby's parents were a few miles offshore in their sailboat trying out some new rigging when they were intercepted by the pirates. Some Catholic friends of his family — a child-less American couple that owned a luxury resort hotel on the beach just outside the capital, Victoria — took Toby in and went on to adopt and raise him.

Thanks to the beautiful witness of charity, humility, and especially forgiveness (they taught Toby to forgive his parent's murderers), given by his new parents, Toby grew to love Jesus. Consequently, when he was 12 years old, Toby converted to Catholicism.

"Toby, how did you learn of this mission?"asked Stuart.

"Last night," replied Toby, "I had a beautiful dream in which I was directed to meet all of you here at the Cathedral this morning. I was in Marrakesh, Morocco, when I had the dream. I was there to shop in a world famous market called the Medina. My parents sent me there to pick out and order rugs, antiques, pottery, and some other items for our family's resort hotel. This morning, I immediately booked a flight to Algiers and met up with Charlie about 15 minutes ago."

Stuart told Charlie and Toby how the Queen communicated with him via *La Imagen Viva* and how the four of us would constitute a mission team. He then turned to Charlie and said that, according to Bella, she, Charlie, would be the one to tell all of us about the next phase of our journey.

"Yes, Scooter, although we all realize that you have been selected to lead the team, the next step in our mission was shared with me because it will take place here in my homeland,

Algeria. We are to go out into the Sahara Desert for a week of formation with Jean-Pierre, my spiritual father.

"Jean-Pierre is an 80-year-old retired bishop from Paris who, rather than following the typical, comfortable lifestyle of a retired french bishop — vacations on the French Riviera, etc... — has chosen to follow in St. Charles de Foucauld's footsteps and live an austere, humble life of prayer and penance in the desert.

"My family owns a small farm in Tamanrasset where we grow and market apricots, almonds, dates, and figs. We also raise and market dromedary camels. My cousin, Justin, works for the family business and lives here in Algiers. Using the small truck he drives for the family business, he will take us to Tamanrasset, which is approximately 1,000 miles from here.

"When we arrive at my family home in Tamanrasset, we'll get together some provisions and, riding four of the six camels I personally raised, head out into the desert to Jean-Pierre's encampment.

"We will also require the services of a burro I raised. His name is Augustine. He's great at carrying gear and he loves to lead a camel caravan. Like Augustine, my camels are named after well-known, Catholic Berbers.

"The camels we will be taking are named Cyprian, Miltiades, Tertullian, and Monica. St. Cyprian was a bishop of Carthage; Miltiades was pope when Emperor Constantine the Great issued the Edict of Milan... which granted Christianity legal status in the Roman Empire; Tertullian, who was the first writer in Latin to use the term 'Trinity,' was a prolific Christian author and apologist who is sometimes referred to as the 'father of Latin Christianity' and the 'founder of Western theology.'

"And last but not least, St. Monica was the mother of perhaps the greatest Church Father of the Patristic period... Augustine.

"St. Augustine, as you probably know, was bishop of Hippo and author of *The City of God*, and... *The Confessions*; an autobiography recounting his life, and especially his conversion to Christianity.

"Oh! Here is my cousin now. I'll sit up front with him and we'll take turns driving. You guys can climb into the back of the truck where there are some cushions so you can get some rest. We will arrive in Tamanrasset in the morning and I'll continue this briefing once we leave Tamanrasset and are on our way to the oasis where Jean-Pierre is based. We will have plenty of time to chat since, by camel, it's a 3-hour journey into the heart of the Sahara."

CHAPTER SEVEN

"Charlie," I said, as we set out into the Sahara on camel-back, "Scooter and I now know a little about Toby, so, before you continue with the briefing, why don't you tell us a bit about yourself."

"Of course," replied Charlie, "I'm 21 years old and just graduated from the University of Algiers with a Bachelor of Arts Degree in Philosophy. Albert Camus, who won the 1957 Nobel Prize in Literature, also studied philosophy at the University of Algiers."

"Camus… " I said, "well-known for his contributions to a controversial philosophical position called… *Absurdism.*"

"Yes, Doc," replied Charlie, "he believed the world was absurd. But most Algerians will tell you that the only thing absurd in this world is Camus' absurdism!"

"Very good, Charlie; I like that!" chimed in Scooter.

"So you have your philosophy degree, Charlie," I said, "now what?"

"My dream, believe it or not," answered Charlie, "is to go to the USA and study graduate level theology at the University of Notre Dame."

"Wow, Charlie," responded Toby with excitement, "I also want to study at Notre Dame! I have already applied and been accepted into the *Kroc Institute International Peace Studies Program* to begin studying for a graduate degree in Global Affairs. It's called an MGA Degree."

"Doc... are you hearing this?" asked Scoot with enthusiasm, "We're a team of 'Domers'!"

"Apparently so, Scooter," I responded happily, "this is really starting to feel like a family reunion!"

"Yes, Toby," replied Charlie, "I also applied and found out just yesterday that I have been accepted into the graduate theology program as an international student... with a full scholarship!"

After congratulating Charlie and Toby, I said:

"Well, Charlie, now that we know more about your life, why don't you continue to brief us regarding this next step in our spiritual journey."

"We will spend a week in silent retreat with Jean-Pierre as our director," began Charlie, "and he will meet with each of us for 30 minutes everyday, and daily with all of us as a group at 3pm for the only full meal of the day. Each of us will have our own little tent. It will be warm in the day, but bearable because our tents will be positioned beneath the shade of a grouping of trees. Jean-Pierre lives in a tiny, two-room adobe dwelling. The personal meetings will take place between 8 and 10 am, outside in the open air beneath a palm tree in front of Jean-Pierre's hermitage. Jean-Pierre likes to meet in that particular spot because it brings to mind the beautiful encounter Abraham had with God when he met with the three mysterious visitors outside his dwelling.

"The communal meeting at 3pm will be in the hermitage where there is a fireplace for cooking as well as a dining table. There is a tiny chapel in one corner of the main room and it's separated from the rest of the room by a heavy, canvas curtain. The name of the tiny chapel is simply... *Jesus in The Desert Chapel.* That's where we will have daily mass at 8pm."

"Charlie," interjected Scooter, "what exactly will this retreat be about?"

"I don't really know, Scooter," returned Charlie, "we will have to wait until we get there and Jean-Pierre tells us. He has been informed by the Spirit regarding our mission, as well as the purpose of our visit to his camp and his role in our formation. I know this much, Scooter: our time with Jean-Pierre will be preparation for everything that is to follow. You could compare it to the time Jesus took three of his disciples to Mt. Tabor to prepare them for his paschal mystery."

"The Transfiguration!" observed Scooter, excitedly.

"Yes," was Charlotte's measured reply, "after a week in the Sahara Desert with Jean-Pierre, you will never be the same."

"Charlie," I said, "I have never ridden a camel before, nor have I ever even been in close proximity to one. But now, I am fascinated with them! Could you possibly tell us something about them?" I inquired.

"Of course." responded Charlie. "As you may have deduced by now, I'm something of a camel expert. I raised the camels we are riding from the time of their birth; so they are very pleasant and responsive. They're happy camels! But not all camels are happy. Some are treated very poorly, and it shows in their temperament and behavior. It is never a good idea to strike a camel in anger; they remember.

"The muslim people of the Sahara know that, although the camel is a large, powerful creature, it is actually very gentle. It is said that on one occasion, the Prophet Muhammad comforted a weeping camel tied to a post in Medina.

"Algeria is the largest country in Africa and the tenth largest country in the world, and the Sahara Desert makes up 90% of Algeria. So, although there is ample space for camels, as you can well imagine, there are *only* around 420 thousand camels, or as they are sometimes referred to… *ships of the desert…* in Algeria; as compared with Somalia, a much smaller nation, that has six million camels!"

"What do they eat?" interjected Scoot.

"They eat pretty much the same thing horses and cattle eat; hay and grass. But because camels had to adapt to a much harsher environment, they can also eat, well… just about anything that grows out in the desert; including thorny bushes, cactuses with their needles, and even dry twigs. The inside of their mouths, and especially their lips, are structured in such a way that enables them to safely eat rough things that other grazing animals could never eat… including the venomous, Saharan

Horned Viper! The powerful chemicals in the camel's digestive system neutralize the viper's venom.

"The hump on their back, contrary to popular belief, is not a water storage tank; it is filled with energy-rich fat which can keep the camel alive when food is scarce. If necessary, camels can go for a couple of weeks without food. And when the fat is used up, the hump flops over like an empty sack. The fact that all their body fat is situated in one place means that the rest of their body, being fat-free, cools off much faster.

"With regard to the camel's hump, dromedary camels have one hump and Bactrian camels have two humps. Bactrian camels tend to be a little bigger than the typical dromedary. The dromedaries are famous because they were the camels used by the three Magi in the Bible. Dromedaries are found in North Africa, the Middle East, and Australia, whereas the Bactrian are mainly found in China and Mongolia.

"Right now, Australia has the largest population of *wild* Arabian camels (dromedaries) in the world. In 1977, Robyn Davidson... the so-called 'camel woman' of Australia... at 26 years old, crossed the vast Great Australian Desert—1,700 miles—with only 4 dromedaries and her faithful little dog named Diggity.

"Her daring adventure was followed by National Geographic and was one of their greatest and most popular stories ever. *Tracks* is the name of a movie that tells the whole wonderful story. But just to keep things in perspective, as big as the

Great Australian Desert is, the Sahara is larger than the entire continent of Australia!

"Camels have three eyelids, one of which is transparent so they can see during a sandstorm without sustaining any damage to their eyes. Not only that; this transparent eyelid also functions as a sort of prescription lens that, if the need arises, enables the camel to see even better than without it."

"Like when they want to read the small print in a camel caravan contract?" joked Scooter.

"Camels would be more likely to *eat* a camel caravan contract than read it, Scooter! But I know you're joking. Also, their feet differ from what one might expect. Unlike horses that have very hard hooves, the bottom of a camel's foot is a big, gelatinous pad that serves them well in the hot, sandy, desert environment. They have two rows of long eyelashes to protect their eyes, and they have thick pads of skin on their chest and knees so they can sit comfortably on the hot sand.

"And with regard to water storage, rather than storing it in any particular place, the red blood cells of the camel expand up to 240% of their original volume so that their entire body can serve as a liquid storage container."

"Wow... Like a walking canteen!" I said, playfully.

"Exactly!" answered Charlie, with a smile.

"You know," said Tobey, "I can't help but reflect on the similarity between how well God prepared camels for their mission, and how he is preparing us for ours."

"Yes, Toby," returned Charlie, "you are right; I can see the similarity as well. Thank you for sharing that beautiful observation."

"Yeah, thanks Toby; what a cool insight!" added Scoot.

"Hey," I said, "a funny thought just came to me. Do you think these camels are destined to be part of our team?"

"It wouldn't surprise me," said Charlie, "they're definitely amazing creatures."

"Well… hold on now, folks," said Scooter, trying to keep a straight face, "if they're going to be part of the team, they're going to have to study at Notre Dame!"

"If need be, I think that could be arranged." I said, while attempting to appear as serious and professional as possible.

After a second or two, all of us burst out laughing at the thought. We were all so cheerful and the trip was going so well, it was hard to believe we were riding camels deep into the legendary and forbidding Sahara Desert.

"Charlie," asked Scooter, "since you are the only one here who knows anything about this area, could you please share with us some of what you know about Charles de Foucauld?"

CHAPTER EIGHT

"Tamanrasset," began Charlie, "is a 4,330 feet high oasis city located in the Ahaggar Mountains, which are surrounded by the Sahara Desert. Tamanrasset was originally a military outpost that was established to protect the trans-Saharan, camel caravan trade routes which intersected in that area. It is also the chief city of the Algerian Tuareg Berbers.

"Charles de Foucauld was born on September 15th, 1858… and he died on December 1st, 1916. He moved to Tamanrasset in French Algeria around 1904, long before the horrendous Algerian War of Independence (1954-1962) was fought against France; the European colonial power that had long since worn out its welcome… if it ever actually had one.

"With regard to this bitter and bloody period in the history of my country, French President Emmanuel Macron, in 2017, characterized the French colonization of Algeria as a *'crime against humanity.'* He went on to say: *'It's truly barbarous and it's part of a past we need to confront by apologizing to those against whom we committed these acts.'*

"In any case, as though God, through the humble, prayerful presence of one saintly man, was preparing and strengthening our people spiritually for the nightmare that would be unleashed on us 38 years after his death, Charles experienced a

deep calling to live among, and become one with, the impove-
rished Berber people.

"He had been a Trappist monk but longed for a life of greater austerity and solitude. He traveled to Palestine in 1897 and
lived in Nazareth for a while where he served as a handyman
and a humble porter for a convent of Poor Clares. Eventually,
he heard the call of the Sahara and came to Tamanrasset to live
among the poor in the desert… with Jesus.

"Abiding in the desert, he was led by the Spirit to evange-
lize not with words or by preaching, but through presence: the
simple witness of a radiant, Christian life of peace and love.
According to what I have heard about him, local information
that has been passed down from one generation to the next, he
lived a humbler and more austere life than most of the inhabi-
tants of Tamanrasset at that time.

"Based on his writings, it would seem that this particular
apostolic approach was something he developed while living
in Nazareth. Jesus lived a quiet, hidden life in Nazareth for 30
years; and we know very little, if anything, about it. And yet it
formed the foundation for an incomparable, unprecedented,
truly salvific and historic ministry of eschatological propor-
tions. So there must have been *something* dynamically spiritual
about those quiet, so-called 'hidden years'.

"Well, Charles discovered there was indeed 'something'—
something wonderful—about a poor, simple, hidden life;
something that could generate a phenomenally profound and

efficacious spiritual communion with the living God. So convinced was he of the inestimable value of this way of life that he was compelled to embrace it with his whole heart and soul.

"This is why the great French Dominican theologian, Yves Congar, speculated that on the threshold of the atomic century, God raised up Charles de Foucauld and Thèrése of Lisieux to remind the world that the real 'power' needed by man rests in God, and can be encountered through the simplicity, humility, and grace of an interior life of loving communion with God; rather than in the horrifying and destructive external manifestations produced by the atomic age. It is as if man is more interested in what is going on inside an atom than with what is going on inside himself.

"Fr. Charles was murdered on December 1st, 1916, by a band of Bedouin tribal raiders. Intending to kidnap him, the desert bandits surrounded his hermitage and forcibly removed him from his dwelling; and that's when their unholy 'plan' went tragically sideways. Two members of the French Camel Cavalry suddenly arrived on the scene and the raiders panicked. Fr. Charles along with the two Camel Corps soldiers were shot dead. Charles was 58 years old.

"But lest you develop a negative view of my country and its wonderful people because of what I have just shared regarding this calamitous incident, I would like to provide some balance by adding the words of John Limbert, a man who was one of the hostages during the infamous 1981 Iran Hostage Crisis—

an international crisis in which Algeria was chosen by both parties to serve as mediator.

"His words were so well stated that I memorized them verbatim. Five years after he was released from captivity, John became the American Ambassador to Algeria. And in 2021, on the fortieth anniversary of the hostage crisis, Ambassador Limbert had this to say:

"'*My family and I will never forget the kindness and hospitality we experienced from the Algerian people. Although 40 years have passed since that fateful day, the kindness and professionalism of Algerian friends remains fresh in my memory. I, for one, will never forget your assistance and friendship. With best wishes to the proud people of this beautiful country...*'"

"Thank you, Charlie," I said in a somewhat solemn tone, "for sharing with us the life of this holy man of God. Hearing his life story from you, and knowing the special connection your family has with this gifted individual, has rendered the entire experience more edifying than any of us could have ever imagined."

"Absolutely!" added Tobey, "Thanks, Charlie. We could not have had a better introduction to the intrepid, adventurous priest who will be watching over us for the duration of our mission."

"Charlie, could you tell us a little more about the connection between Charles and Jean-Pierre?" asked Scoot.

"Jean-Pierre's parents," began Charlie, "were very fond of the spirituality presented in a well-known book from the 18th century titled... *Abandonment To Divine Providence.* It was written by a devout, French Jesuit named Jean Pierre de Caussade. They held this Jesuit in such high esteem that they named their son after him.

"So you could say Bishop Jean-Pierre was raised in the shadow of this great, French spiritual writer, who also happened to be renowned as a spiritual director. Is it any wonder therefore that Jean-Pierre is also known to be an exceptional spiritual director."

"So it's almost as though we will be spending a week praying in the desert with Caussade!" added Tobey, filled with wonder.

"Yes," responded Charlie in confirmation, "but there is more. Brother Charles, as he preferred to be called, like Caussade, had deep insight into the spirituality of abandonment. Charles' *Prayer of Abandonment* is extremely popular with young people today and, in general, is probably better known by our contemporaries than Caussade's celebrated treatise.

"I should also add that Jean-Pierre has continued with and further developed Br. Charles' reflections on the hidden years in Nazareth, and he sees in them a profound teaching on abandonment to divine providence. For 30 years, Jesus lived a simple life as a faithful, loving member of a poor, humble family. And for all those years, he was completely at peace, always trusting that his Father would guide him regarding the where, when, and how of his salvific mission.

"Jean-Pierre was so moved by this profound manifestation of trinitarian love that he named his encampment in the desert… *Little Nazareth.*"

"Hey, Charlie," asked Scoot carefully, trying not to appear overly concerned, "not to shift gears too abruptly, but there's one final question we 'foreigners'—Doc, Tobey, and myself—would like to run by you; what do you think we will be eating during this retreat?"

"Lots of couscous, of course." replied Charlie, "That's the national dish of Algeria. Often, the couscous will be topped with a tasty stew composed of lamb and local vegetables. We will also have plenty of Kesra; a flat bread made from semolina and cooked in a cast iron pan. It is the most popular bread in Algeria. Kesra is very nice in the morning, hot and covered with cinnamon, wild honey and raisins.

"There will also be delicious fresh dates, figs, apricots, and almonds on hand in various presentations at every meal. I hope you like tea because Algerian Mint Tea is one of the main things we will be drinking at the encampment."

"The menu sounds fantastic, Charlie!" I said.

"Oh, you will not be disappointed. Everything is fresh, natural, wholesome, and delectable. Also, you will notice that the heat tends to calm down the appetite and, consequently, this will free us up and enable us to focus more on prayer.

"Well, my friends, we are almost there. When we reach the top of that little rise up ahead, you will be able to see the oasis in the distance."

CHAPTER NINE

After approximately three hours traversing an almost invisible trail through the scorching, barren desert, with each of us 'foreigners' dressed in typical berber fashion to avoid any undue attention should there be any bandits in the area, and having allowed our hair and beards to grow out in an attempt to enculturate and fit in, we arrived at the oasis.

Within minutes, we found ourselves 'parked' in front of Jean-Pierre's humble, adobe dwelling. Augustine was noticeably proud of himself, standing tall with his head raised high, as if to say… "There; how's *that* for leadership!"

"Welcome to *Little Nazareth*," said Jean-Pierre, calmly, with a gentle smile, "how was your trip? Uneventful, I hope. I have been praying for you all morning. You must be hungry. Please, come into my humble home… dinner is ready and waiting."

Jean-Pierre was a tall, thin man, standing at around six foot, three inches and weighing around 170 pounds. He was wearing a long, bedouin style white tunic that draped over his camel hide sandals, a floppy, wide-brimmed canvas hat, and a simple, hand-carved wooden pectoral cross. He was a gentle, peaceful man with long, flowing white hair who, when speaking with you, would, from time to time, close his eyes in order to listen more closely to your heart and soul. The whole impression this created was that of being in the presence of one of the ancient patriarchs.

This habit of closing his eyes while listening took a little getting used to. At first, it seemed as though he was about to fall asleep. But after a couple of days we realized it was just his way of listening.

Jean-Pierre was not one to move about very much. When he took up a position in a chair, or on the ground outside, he would stay there for an hour... or two... or three! And when he did move from one place to the next, he did so in complete silence... as if he were weightless.

This also took some getting used to. Occasionally, he would come up from behind and you wouldn't hear a thing until he tapped you on the shoulder, or said "hello." Strangely enough, however, this sort of thing was not as startling as it should have been since, by all accounts, under "normal" circumstances, one should have practically gone into cardiac arrest. But there was a mysterious, deep peace at *Little Nazareth* that permeated each of us to such a degree that nothing short of a sudden strike by a desert horned viper would have been able to startle us.

The dinner conversation, at Jean-Pierre's request, focused mainly upon each of us sharing a little more about ourselves so he could get to know us better. Following dinner, the whole tone of our gathering morphed into something truly beautiful.

It was no longer a conversation but rather a privileged moment in which a spiritual master began teaching his young students.

Jean-Pierre moved quietly to a central position in front of the fireplace where there was a low, simple wooden chair draped with a fluffy, white sheepskin. On the floor in front of the chair was a light brown, handwoven berber camel hair rug with four large floor pillows scattered about.

Each of us sat upon one of the pillows and turned to face our serene mentor, Jean-Pierre, who was at that point sitting motionless, eyes closed and hardly breathing. After around ten minutes of total silence… which, due to the great anticipation we had of hearing him speak, seemed more like an hour… he opened his eyes, raised his right hand to chest level directly in front of his pectoral cross, and in a tone of voice just a bit louder than a whisper, made the sign of the cross and said:

"The blessing of almighty God; Father, Son, and Holy Spirit, descend upon you and remain with you forever. This has been your first teaching; how to be still and silent in the presence of God… who, while being transcendent, has chosen to live within you! I am not your formator; God is your formator. I am just a lowly teacher who will share some things with you that I have learned over the years regarding prayer and the interior life. We will meet again in the chapel at 8pm for holy mass. Following mass, I will give a teaching on quiet, interior prayer.

"I should also mention that Athanasius, one of Charlie's relatives who lives here in the oasis and assists me when I have guests, will stop by your tents, sometimes accompanied by his

wife or one of his six children, at 6:30pm every evening with tea,
Algerian goat cheese, bread and fresh fruit. He will do the same
thing at 7:30am every morning. I hope you will be able to settle
in now and get some rest after your long journey."

Thus began a truly remarkable experience none of us will
soon forget. That evening, I helped Jean-Pierre set up for the
mass, and I asked him when he was going to give us the details
regarding our mission. He said he would wait for the final day
of the retreat to inform us because if he told us now, it would
present an unnecessary distraction during this precious time
of spiritual development.

That first mass was so extraordinarily beautiful and sublime, all of us felt as though we were attending mass for the
first time. The sense we had was that we were present at the
last supper and it wasn't Jean-Pierre offering the mass... it was
Jesus himself. Jean-Pierre wore a simple, beige, camel hair
chasuble that was handmade right there in the oasis by Athanasius' wife.

In the center of the chest area was a hand-embroidered,
lifesize heart bearing the wound from the lance that had pierced it, with a few drops of blood flowing out of the wound onto
the chasuble. It was an extremely powerful image and perfectly
in sync with the holy sacrifice.

In lieu of a homily, Jean-Pierre simply picked up the open
book of the Gospels and drew it close to his chest where it covered the embroidered, pierced heart of Jesus, as well as his

own heart. And then, in a tender tone of voice one might expect from an angel, he said:

"God is love, and his Word is love outpoured!"

As if all of this was not a profound enough spiritual experience to process in the course of one day, the teaching on prayer that followed was sufficiently elevated to cause us to believe we had actually died with Jesus during the mass and were now enjoying the risen life with him in heaven.

CHAPTER TEN

Following the mass, we relocated to our "classroom" in front of the fireplace and took up our positions on the floor pillows while Jean-Pierre settled into the sheepskin-covered, rustic wooden chair. Then he carefully picked up a ten-inch long crucifix that was lying on the top of a small wooden crate beside his chair. He gazed lovingly at the crucifix for a moment, raised it to his lips and kissed it.

Then, with great devotion, he pressed the heart of Jesus crucified to his breast. After this deeply moving manifestation of interior love, he returned the crucifix to its original place atop the crate beside his chair. Finally, in a soft tone of voice that was barely audible... with eyes half closed... he began to speak:

"Prayer is more important than eating or sleeping. Prayer is life, because prayer is Jesus and Jesus is life. When you pray, it is Jesus himself who is praying in you.

"Each of you has a nicely developed prayer life; which is one of the main reasons you were selected for this special assignment. Nevertheless, there is room for growth; and there will always be room for growth. Why? Because prayer is relational; it's a personal relationship between the individual and the three divine persons... Father, Son, and Holy Spirit.

"Therefore, since it is a personal relationship, it will, ideally, always be deepening and developing... just like all personal relationships. Unfortunately, just as we observe with too many human relationships, a person's prayer life can stagnate and come to a complete halt. This cessation of development is commonly referred to as 'lukewarmness.'

"The issue here is that the spiritually lukewarm individual does not simply coast along on a spiritual plateau. If the prayer life/relationship is not growing and developing, it is almost always diminishing.

"Fortunately, none of you has this problem. You were brought here to the desert because God saw your heart's desire to grow in prayerful communion with him. Ask, and you shall receive; seek, and you will find. What father would give his child a scorpion when he asks for an egg? How much more will your Heavenly Father give the Holy Spirit to those who ask! (Luke 11:12-13)

"The first form of prayer we learn is vocal prayer. As children, we learn to say our prayers. Then, as we grow and learn how to read, we are able to not simply recite our memorized prayers but also to read them. In time, as we develop the capacity to read scripture and other inspirational writings, we begin to enter into a new way of prayer called meditation, in which the mind ponders deeply that which has been read, seen, or imagined. The rosary is a form of meditation that also incorporates vocal prayer.

"Many people who are living a virtuous and devout life reach this level of prayer. The problem is they believe this to be the final stage of prayer and the culmination of the spiritual life. It isn't; it's actually a sort of 'spiritual launching pad;' there is more... much more! The development and growth must continue because prayer is a real, personal relationship, not some sort of spiritual/psychological state that provides the person with a controllable level of religious comfort; a 'spiritual comfort zone' that gives a sense of security... while at the same time pacifying the demands of one's conscience.

"Rather than getting hung up on the launching pad, each of you has moved through meditation to quiet, interior prayer; this is what has led you here to the desert. My role now is to teach you a way to continue growing in this new, spiritual development you have been gifted with. The 'way' I am going to show you will provide the discipline required to enter ever more deeply into this beautiful gift of silent, interior prayer of the heart.

"When I began this teaching you watched me gently lift up the crucifix, gaze at it reverently, kiss it, then lovingly press the heart of Jesus against my own heart. Jesus crucified is the gateway to wordless, interior prayer, and this is the way you will begin your daily period of contemplative encounter with the God who dwells within you. The crucified one is the only 'Word' you will need when you enter into the mysterious, peaceful silence of your heart. I call this way of silent prayer I developed here in the desert... The Prayer of Jesus Crucified.

"Charlotte, you may now pass out the crucifixes I asked you to pick up in Algiers and bring to this meeting."

Charlotte opened the leather satchel containing the four crucifixes and handed one to each of us, saying as she did so... "Peace be with you." Clearly handmade, the crucifixes were simple, but magnificent! "Each of these," continued Charlie, "was crafted using raw, unfinished Saharan Cypress wood that was cut around 100 years ago; long before the species was endangered and now protected."

She went on to tell how the Saharan Cypress (*Cupressus dupreziana*) is listed by *The International Union for the Conservation of Nature* as one of Earth's rarest tree species. The corpus on the wood cross, Charlie pointed out, was carved from camel bone by local artisans and hand painted with colors made from indigenous plants. Then Jean-Pierre began to explain the significance of these particular materials:

"The tree most capable of not only surviving, but most capable also of thriving in extremely arid conditions is the Saharan Cypress. And as you have witnessed, the animal most suited and adapted for living in an extremely dry environment is the camel.

"It was for these reasons that a friend of Charlotte's who is an admirer of Fr. Foucauld's spirituality chose these materials when he fashioned the crucifixes you are now holding in your hands. Silent, interior prayer is the 'driest' of all prayer forms, and therefore, as I'm sure you have already discovered, it is almost always a spiritually arid experience.

"If you are ever tempted to think your daily contemplative prayer is useless, or 'not working'... your crucifix will remind you not to give up but to recognize that a deeper spiritual life is hidden in the dryness and the aridity. The arid, desert experience of contemplative prayer gives birth to a whole new level of communion with God.

"Contemplative prayer is not based on feelings; it is rooted in the will. Often, people will come to the erroneous conclusion that they are not ready for quiet prayer since whenever they attempt it, they find their mind filled with distractions and worldly concerns. This state of cognitive preoccupation, however, is really quite normal. It does not in itself constitute a barrier to interior prayer of the heart.

"Contemplative prayer is all about the will and the heart; the mind is of little importance. As St. Teresa of Avila pointed out:

'The soul is not the mind, nor is the will directed by thinking, for this would be very unfortunate. Hence, the soul's progress does not lie in thinking much, but in loving much.'

"In quiet prayer, the individual enters into the mysterious serenity of the mind of Christ and discovers a peace that has nothing to do with the world; this is one of the reasons for the experience of dryness and aridity."

Jean-Pierre concluded his outline of interior prayer by inviting us to take advantage of this unique period of solitude by
spending three hours a day in silent prayer; an hour in the
morning, an hour in the afternoon, and an hour in the evening.
He explained how commitment and discipline are more important for the development of the contemplative stage of prayer than for any of the other stages that precede it. As one's
prayer life simplifies, the discipline required to cooperate with
this gifted development increases accordingly.

In addition, he pointed out how, historically, something similar to what happened with scripture seems to have also happened with prayer. Just as it was thought that since the faithful
lacked the appropriate theological training they should not be
encouraged to read the Word of God, so, too, since they lacked
the spiritual formation thought to be required, they were not
encouraged to engage in contemplative prayer.

Both these practices were considered to be "safe" only in
the hands of the initiated... that is, in the hands of clerics and
members of religious orders.

The issue regarding scripture was addressed successfully in
recent years and is no longer a problem. But the hesitancy regarding quiet, wordless prayer has proven to be deeper and
more difficult to resolve.

The Second Vatican Council spoke to this question with its
famous proclamation of the *Universal Call to Holiness*. The
implication being that *all* the faithful were invited and encouraged to employ, without exception, *all* the means available in

the tradition to pursue growth and development in holiness…
unto Transforming Union itself.

Although this was indeed a great start in addressing a long
standing spiritual deficit, much more needs to be done at the
pastoral level, as well as in seminaries.

CHAPTER ELEVEN

Each of us received numerous gifts and blessings in the days of serenity following that unforgettable introduction to contemplative, desert spirituality. The movements of the Spirit in the depths of the soul, if welcomed and nurtured in the context of a disciplined and ascetical predisposition, can bring the person into a profound state of wonder and communion that is as mysterious as it is transforming.

Scooter experienced this sort of thing one afternoon and spoke to Jean-Pierre about it that evening. Employing a dramatic, serious tone, which was somewhat out of character for Scoot, he explained how, while strolling about the oasis to get a bit of air, he suddenly found himself completely immersed in God. He had not been praying nor was he consciously thinking of God. In a relaxed, rather nonchalant manner, Jean-Pierre responded thusly:

"That's wonderful, Stuart... a great sign! We have a name for this type of spiritual experience; we call it a 'Bubble.' You were taken into God and it was as though you were in the world, but no longer of the world. Correct?

Nodding his head vigorously, Scoot affirmed Jean-Pierre's succinct description... while the rest of us just sat there filled with amazement. Feeling encouraged by Scoot's trust and openness, Charlie shared something that was truly wonderful.

She said that, like Scooter, when she was not focused on God but was busy arranging things in her tent, she suddenly found herself immersed in "light;" light that was unlike any light that is found in this world. This spiritual light seemed to be coming from within and without at the same time. So unique was this experience that she was sure she had, in some mysterious way, entered into heaven itself.

Immediately following upon the arrival of this heavenly light, she was able to sense clearly and distinctly the loving presence of the three divine persons... Father, Son, and Holy Spirit. She was not sure how long the experience lasted because time stood still while she was caught up in this celestial encounter.

Afterwards, she was left in what she described as a state of holy stupor, in which all she could do was ponder the unfathomable goodness of God. She went on to explain how this experience had filled her with such a remarkably deep peace and tranquility that, had a rabid hyena stepped inside the doorway of her tent, she would have, without hesitation, stooped down and planted a big kiss directly atop his wild, furry head!

Needless to say, after hearing of this incredible, spiritual occurrence, we were all rendered speechless as we sat there motionless... in an elevated state of wonder. A few seconds passed, when, not surprisingly, and in unison, all eight eyes slowly turned toward Jean-Pierre... breathlessly awaiting his response.

"What you have just heard Charlie describe so well, a mystical experience of the Triune God, is a central part of the highest development of prayer known as... Transforming Union.

"In her opus magnum, The Interior Castle, St. Teresa of Avila... Doctor of the Church and Teacher of Prayer... pointed out that in the most advanced stage of prayer... the seventh mansion (or in Spanish... the seventh 'morada'):

'The soul sees these three persons individually, and
yet, by a wonderful kind of knowledge which is given
to it, the soul realizes that most certainly and truly all
these three Persons are one Substance, one Power,
one Knowledge, and one God alone.'

I also had an interior happening I never experienced before, but was hesitant to share it with the team out of fear of degrading the retreat into a sort of spiritual competition. Nevertheless, I felt the bonding that was taking place by sharing these precious experiences was more important to the ultimate success of our mission than my pessimistic speculation.

"I had a beautiful experience, Jean-Pierre, that I would like to run by you;" I began, "One evening, when I was walking from my tent to the chapel, I heard these words resound within me: *'You are a temple of the Holy Spirit.'*

"I did not hear the words with my ears, because the voice was not external to me; it was coming from some mysterious place within me, but was, nonetheless, perfectly clear. And I immediately knew, with absolute certainty, the voice was not a product of my imagination and the person speaking was the Father."

As if to confirm the efficacy of my decision to share, Toby ran right through what at that point must have seemed like a wide open door with a big *Welcome* mat in front of it:

"Yes, yes, I had a very similar experience, Dr. Laughton!" exclaimed Toby, with great excitement, "I woke up one morning at around 7am and was just lying there on my cot, fully awake and not thinking about anything in particular, when suddenly I heard someone speaking within me: *'I love you... and I am with you.'*

"I knew beyond a doubt it was the Mother of God who was speaking to me. I just continued to lay there, completely tranquilized by those words from our Mother, while pondering the wonder and the mystery of our life in God."

Radiant with pastoral love, Jean-Pierre gazed at me and Toby for a moment, and then said:

"This experience you had is called a locution. Teresa teaches that the sixth morada, which is often accompanied by locutions, is where the spiritual betrothal occurs. This is, without question, a very good place to be, since, as Teresa points out, the fifth, sixth, and seventh moradas are all associated with the prayer of union... the ultimate development of mystical prayer.

"*I am at this moment, and I suspect all of you are as well, very rejoiced to see what God is doing with you. Clearly, you are on the right path, and clearly you are in the right place. And so, the famous Latin maxim, age quod agis... 'continue doing what you are doing'... applies here.*

"*You would, however, be wise to reflect on how Teresa insisted that the soul could not enter into the fullness of transforming union without having perfect love for one's neighbor. Now you may return to your tents in peace... He is with you!*"

CHAPTER TWELVE

On the third day of our sojourn in the Sahara, something truly lovely took place. As was mentioned earlier, Charlie's valiant burro... Augustine... fashioned himself to be the leader of our caravan. Therefore, or so it seemed, he imagined the only fitting place for him to be stationed was directly in front of the tent belonging to the other, less important leader; Stuart... leader of the mission team.

And so, from day one, he insisted on sleeping at the entrance to Stuart's tent. Scooter woke up on day three and, as was his custom, while remaining on his cot, used his foot to draw open the tent's entrance flap so he could check on the "real leader" of the team... Augustine. Scoot said Augustine was still lying down, but there was something unusual about his posture; his head was raised higher than normal. Upon further examination, Stuart noticed something that looked like a pair of ears sticking up between Augustine's extended front legs.

He sat up to get a better look, and there, sleeping peacefully and nestled lovingly between Augustine's forelimbs, was the national animal of Algeria; a very young Fennec Fox. The kit was a reynard (male) around two months old and weighed about a pound and a half. With its signature outsized ears...

that appeared to be on loan from Yoda... this wonderful little creature was as cute as can be imagined. The whole scene was truly heartwarming; a friendly burro protecting and comforting a frightened and vulnerable kit, whose mother was probably killed by a jackal.

Stuart rose carefully from his cot, not wanting to startle the young, traumatized creature. As he exited the tent, he purposely avoided eye contact with the kit, hoping to appear as if he didn't see it. Not knowing that much about the Fennec Fox, he then proceeded to Charlie's tent to consult with her regarding how they should deal with Augustine's new friend. Charlie was astounded and said:

"This is amazing, Scooter! This is only the second time in my entire life I have heard of a Fennec kit seeking refuge among humans. I can tell you right now that this kit has been sent to be part of our team. I don't know how I know this, but if you realized how rare such an occurrence is, you also would sense providence at work here. The poor creature is probably starving, so the first order of business would be to try and feed it. But before we do that, we should have a suitable way to refer to it. Since you were the one to discover it, have you thought of a name for it?"

"Yes," replied Scooter, "I would like his name to be... Alypius."

"Forgive my ignorance, Scooter," responded Charlie, "but who is, or was, Alypius?"

"Alypius of Thagaste. Thagaste was an ancient city in what is now Algeria. Alypius was a lifelong friend of St. Augustine. When Augustine converted to Christianity, his friend Alypius converted along with him. Augustine mentions their friendship a number of times in his autobiography... *The Confessions*.

"Alypius was actually present in the garden at Milan when Augustine had the mysterious experience that brought about his conversion. In 387, he and Augustine were baptized together by Ambrose at the Easter Vigil. After his baptism, Alypius assisted Augustine in founding the first monastery in Northern Africa. Then, in 394, Alypius was named Bishop of Thagaste."

"Wonderful, Stuart... fantastic choice; I love it!" replied Charlie with a big smile. "Well... now that we have a dignified name for our newest team member, let's get a few things together to feed Alypius. One should never feed a Fennec Fox processed foods, only whole foods. Things such as insects, eggs, fruit, birds, mice, geckos, or any raw meat. But since he is still a kit, let's begin by bringing Alypius fresh water, a few dates, and an egg."

Alypius turned out to be as friendly to us as Augustine was to him. It was readily apparent that he would be a great blessing to the team. One gift we benefited from immediately was his super hearing. He could hear a desert horned viper as it moved cautiously through the sand twenty-five yards away. When he detected one, he would extend his ears to maximum height… as if each of his ears was a radar tower… turn them in the direction of the approaching danger, and alert the community with a series of threatening growls. If a benign animal such as a sheep or a chicken was drawing near to our encampment, Alypius would sound an alert with a couple of friendly barks.

All things considered, we found ourselves wondering whether Augustine may have actually been aware of the Fennec Fox's gift of hearing, and welcomed him… or should I say *recruited* him… because he knew the fox would serve as a magnificent security system and would be a true asset to our team.

We came to the conclusion that our little hypothesis was not out of the question since Augustine was born and raised in the Sahara and over the years had many encounters with Fennec Foxes. Charlie said Augustine was approached once by an entire skulk of ten Fennec Foxes who had picked up the scent of the various food items he was transporting in the cargo baskets strapped to his back.

Charlie went on to relate how Augustine had been a bit annoyed by their presence, but not frightened, since a mature Fennec Fox, weighing around three pounds, is smaller than the notoriously courageous Mexican Chihuahua. A full-grown Chihuahua generally weighs in at around five pounds.

Charlie said that when the skulk surrounded Augustine, she got down from her camel, took some food from the baskets Augustine was carrying, walked ten yards away from the caravan, and fed the hungry foxes. Augustine witnessed this beautiful act of compassion and respect for our Father's innocent creatures. And chances are, he was impressed and never forgot it.

CHAPTER THIRTEEN

On the day before we were scheduled to leave *Little Nazareth*, Jean-Pierre asked us to meet with him before the main meal for a special session:

"My little ones... tomorrow I will be sending you out like sheep among wolves. But I am not afraid for you; I fear for the wolves! You have done so well during this period of formation in the desert... giving yourselves over completely to the love of God... that you will find yourselves immersed in such an abundance of wondrous gifts that only a complete fool would dare attempt to block you as you work toward the completion of your special mission.

"Before you arrived, the Spirit indicated that specific information regarding your mission would be given to me, and it has been; the Spirit has indeed graciously illuminated my mind. You will be going to Manhattan, New York City. You will be traveling there on the Rocinante; *the same vintage tramp steamer that brought you to Algeria. It just so happens that as the crew was preparing the ship to leave the port in Algiers, they discovered a serious problem with the engine and have been delayed waiting for replacement parts.*

"You will be taking your animals with you; they are an important part of your mission team. As to what you will be doing

in New York City... that is, what exactly is the mission... I don't know. The actual mission will be revealed to Scooter little by little, on site, as circumstances present themselves. Your mission will 'unfold' in the Spirit. You will not know what it is until it is upon you.

"This is a protection for you because, if you knew what was being asked of you, you would consider it to be utterly impossible and would be tempted to shy away. And that would not be an unreasonable response because, the truth is; it will be impossible... for you; but not for God.

"God will give you every gift you need to complete this important mission. And like the mission itself, he will give you the gift at the exact time you need it. All of these gifts will be rooted in love, not in power... understood in a worldly way. When you are faced with obstacles and challenges, do not lose faith, do not give way to fear. With the grace of God you will overcome all of them.

"You are living in the Spirit now. At times, you may feel like you are 'floating' above the world, because... you will be! When you are moving in Christ, the world and everything in it are laid at your feet. You will see all things through his eyes.

"You will want to keep in mind that due to this oneness with God which you have been raised to through Transforming Union, you will radiate the eternal life and love of the three divine persons everywhere you go and with everyone you encounter. This will generate within you immeasurable peace and joy.

"It would be remiss of me if I did not suggest that you be very careful not to lose your interior prayer life in the midst of the external happenings you will find yourselves involved in. It is not likely you will have as many opportunities for contemplative solitude as you have had here in the desert. Nevertheless, the Lord will provide space for recollection and quiet prayer sufficient for each day. This development in grace you have been gifted with is integral to your mission.

"All of you have noticed the rapid, shocking decline of morality and spirituality in western civilization. And you have observed how commentators will often ask... 'What has happened to our society?' But it is not really a question of... 'What has happened?'. The real question we should be asking is... 'What has not *happened?'*

"And what is it that has not happened? Spiritual growth! In too many ways, the affluent, super-developed West has become complacent and satisfied with a degree of spiritual life that is relatively shallow, and, therefore, acceptable to an increasingly secularized society. Maintaining the status quo has become the unspoken, spiritual default mindset. But the love of God... if it is anything at all... is fire and passion; and its depth is not determined by minimalistic, worldly standards.

"On the contrary, God's love is *the standard for the world, in that its object is the transformation of the world and everyone in it. And so, as I mentioned to you on your first day here, a*

spiritual life that is not growing… is regressing; and this is a big part of what we are witnessing in our world today.

"As you journey, and as you ponder the wonders of the spiritual life, please keep in mind that no amount of prayer can replace the Eucharist; all good things come forth from that blessed altar, and those same things will return there.

"And to wrap up, now that you know where you are going and how you will get there, all that remains is for you to nurture the inner stillness you discovered here in the desert; that will allow you to be guided and moved by the Spirit. The rest… the mission… will flow peacefully from your intimate communion with God."

After dinner, Scoot and Charlie set about constructing something resembling a throne that could be strapped on Augustine's back so his new assistant, Alypius, would be able to ride along comfortably in the caravan. They made some custom alterations to a small but sturdy basket and introduced a little, homemade camel-hair cushion. They even went so far as to fabricate a removable sun-shield above the throne to protect the young celebrity… *Algeria's National Animal!*

With the addition of Alypius to our team, our caravan was upgraded and entered into the modern, high-tech era of radar. With Alypius poised at the helm on his elevated throne, we would be alerted immediately with regard to any approaching danger. His industrial-sized ears served as a natural form of radar that made all of us feel much more at ease.

The following morning, the day of our departure, we said our goodbyes and began the journey back to Tamanrasset. We must have been quite a sight to contemplate; three college students, one university professor, four camels, one burro, and a Fennec Fox, missioned in the Spirit from the heart of the Sahara Desert to the busiest metropolis in the world... New York City! The epicenter of materialism, hedonism, consumerism, elitist globalism... and the culture of death.

But as much as we were hoping our caravan would have an uneventful crossing of the desert to Tamanrasset... that did not happen; it was as eventful as eventful can be!

CHAPTER FOURTEEN

We were about an hour out from Tamanrasset when Alypius started barking. At first, it was just a little bark every twenty seconds or so. Then he stood on all fours and began barking loud and continuously while aiming his ears in the direction of the approaching danger.

We stopped the caravan and peered into the distance. At around five hundred yards, there was a small group of people on horseback riding quickly in our direction. Charlie said they had probably mistaken us for a caravan they were planning to meet up with.

Then our noble leader, Scooter, spoke up:

"Something is wrong; I don't like the way this feels. Be prepared for anything."

With that alert, Stuart began chanting the *Salve Regina* in Latin:

"Salve Regina, mater misericordiae; vita dulcedo…"

The rest of us joined in, knowing we were not alone and would be given the strength and the gifts to face whatever it was we were about to be confronted with.

As the riders drew closer, we were able to count five. But there was something unusual; two of them had rifles displayed and ready for use. Charlie said this was not normal and clearly a bad sign. The possibility they were bandits was now very much in play.

Toby questioned the bandit theory asking why they would target people who possess nothing of value. Charlie responded:

"Sometimes, all they want are the animals. But in our case, they may be targeting Doc and Scooter... the Americans. Out here in the middle of the Sahara, the possibility of kidnapping Americans for ransom is rare. But when the opportunity arises, it would be difficult for most bandits to resist. Remember... the Bedouin raiders who killed Fr. Charles had originally intended to kidnap him, and he was French; you are American... an even greater ransom could be procured."

"Yes," responded Scooter, "but they would then have to live with the terrifying likelihood of being terminated by Navy Seals in the middle of the night!"

The five horsemen lined up directly in front of our caravan with their leader/spokesman taking the central position. He was brandishing a pistol while the two men occupying the outer edges of the grouping had their rifles shouldered and aimed at us. The remaining two had their handguns holstered, but at the ready.

The four of us, as a natural, unplanned response, formed a similar grouping with Augustine and Alypius taking the center position. Not wasting a moment of his time, and with a harsh, matter of fact tone, the leader of this hostile group of raiders began to speak:

"We know who you are and where you are going. Two of you will not be continuing on to Tamanrasset. Dr. Laughton and Stuart McKenzie… you will be coming with us, back to our camp. From this point on you are our prisoners."

"Who are you to arrest us? We have done nothing wrong!" Stuart responded, thinking they may be associated with the police.

"You are not in a position to question us. Do as I say and no one will get hurt," declared the bandit kidnapper.

At this alarming juncture, with a commanding voice that startled everyone, Charlie, addressing the five horses, shouted out:

"Go home NOW! Run! As fast as you can! GO!!!"

Immediately, all five horses reared up, wheeled around, and took off at a full gallop in the direction they came from. The riflemen and their leader dropped their weapons in a desperate effort to hold on to their horses, and the leader was left dangling along the side of his horse, backwards and upside down, with both hands bouncing across the sand.

The three of us turned and stared at Charlie in total amazement.

"Charlie," I asked, "what just happened here?"

"Right on the spot," answered an excited Charlie, "the Lord gave me the ability to communicate with his creatures! I knew intuitively the gift was being offered for our protection, and so I used it! But having just now witnessed how effective it was… I am as astonished as you!"

"Yes, Charlie," said Stuart, "but all of us have been observing the special way you have with animals, so it makes sense that God would give you, and not one of us, this particular gift. We are so glad you didn't doubt, but chose instead to trust and embrace the gift."

"Hey," interjected Toby, pointing to something in the sand around twenty yards away, "What's that?"

"It looks like it may be something that fell out of the leader's clothing when he went topsy-turvy. Let's check it out." answered Stuart.

It was an envelope containing a piece of paper with Doc and Stuart's name written on it, as well as the date we would be leaving the oasis en route to Tamanrasset.

"Incredible!" exclaimed Scooter, "Look at this; someone gave those raiders this information. But who would betray us in this way?"

"Maybe somebody at the oasis?" offered Toby, "Perhaps, although I hesitate to say it... Athanasius? He was always around and certainly knew our names and our plans."

"I can assure you, it was not Athanasius," said Charlie, "But it may have been someone Athanasius spoke with. He knows everyone in the oasis and is very social. And he was not directed to be discreet regarding our visit to Little Nazareth. So he probably would have shared our names and plans with anyone who inquired. That could explain how such accurate information reached the bandits. Someone associated with one of the bandits may have simply asked Athanasius the right questions and passed his answers on."

"Everything Jean-Pierre said would take place is beginning to happen," commented Scooter. "He told us we would meet with opposition... and we just did. He said he feared more for those who opposed us because of how the Lord might deal with them... and we have just witnessed that as well. Personally, I feel animated and strengthened by this encounter. I hope you also feel inspired and encouraged."

"I do, Scoot," said Toby, "but I would just add that, at this point, your 'scared of Navy Seals' theory is pretty much out the window!"

"Agreed," responded Scoot with a smile, "I concede; fair point, to be sure!"

After we regained our calm and regrouped spiritually, we continued on with our missionary caravan to Tamanrasset. Waiting there for us upon our arrival was Charlie's cousin, Justin. He had everything ready for our overnight trip to the port in Algiers. The truck was gassed up and a suitable livestock trailer securely attached.

When we were all set to move out, we realized there was one more important decision to be made; should Alypius ride in the trailer with his buddy, Augustine? Or would he be safer riding in the cab with us. And how would Augustine and Alypius react to this separation?

We decided the trailer made no sense for tiny Alypius since, due to his diminutive stature, unlike the larger passengers, he could exit the trailer on a whim. So we brought him into the cab with the five of us. Alypius seemed fine with the arrangement, but Augustine, his guardian, shook his head and gave a couple of snorts to express his concern and displeasure.

Once on the road, all of us, including our personal menagerie of innocent creatures, fell fast asleep.

CHAPTER FIFTEEN

As we sailed through the Strait of Gibraltar, an unusual part of the world to be sure, with the ancient Phoenecian port city of Tangier, Morocco, to our south; the UK (Gibraltar itself is a British Overseas Territory), and Spain to our north (Spain *also* to our south in the Spanish autonomous city of Ceuta, on the north African coast and formerly belonging to Morocco), and the great, North Atlantic Ocean directly in front of us... we were filled with a sense of excitement knowing that the city to which we were being sent would be our next stop. New York City was now a mere 3,148 nautical miles away!

During our transatlantic crossing we had ample time to pray, rest, converse, and bond as a team. Being the elder of the group with the most life experience, I had been wondering if something might be developing between the three young college graduates. After all, these were three vibrant young people working closely together while sharing profound spiritual experiences and the greatest adventure any of them had ever had.

What if Stuart and Toby were both developing feelings for Charlie, and Charlie, for her part, was experiencing feelings for one of the young men in particular. If these feelings ever came to light, how would the young man whose romantic feelings were not recognized take it? If such a scenario should come to pass, how would it affect the integrity of our team? Would the persons involved have the maturity to deal with the situation in an acceptable way?

I believed they did have the personal and spiritual maturity to negotiate effectively whatever feelings might arise in the course of our mission. One day, my concerns along these lines were alleviated when I overheard Stuart speaking with Toby and both of them referred to Charlie as… "our sister."

Conversely, a day later, during a conversation I had with Charlie, she referred to Stuart and Toby as… "my brothers." These observations confirmed my hope that the Spirit was keeping the hearts of my youthful comrades focused on the mission.

Indeed, so intense was our focus that we spent the ten days on the high seas in much the same mode as we were in during our sojourn in the desert. As was said so well by the music group, America, in their hit song, A Horse With No Name… *"The ocean is a desert with its life underground and the perfect disguise above;"* the vast, open seascape provided a most con-ducive context for prolonged periods of deep, contemplative prayer.

We also took this blessed opportunity to adapt and equip our custom made crucifixes with a narrow band of leather so they could be worn around the neck, over our traditional Ber-ber tunics.

One afternoon, Toby and Charlie asked me and Stuart if we could lead them down into the hold to visit *La Imagen Viva*. We explained how the Queen had indicated her role in the mission was over, and we had discerned it was her way of saying we should not return to her but continue to move forward. They understood and marveled at the Queen's wisdom.

But that is not to say *La Imagen Viva* had gone into retirement because something quite mysterious did take place out in the middle of the North Atlantic. One day following lunch, the Captain, who tended to relate more to me than the others since we were close in age and I was his brother's friend, asked if he could have a word with me and to follow him to the bow of the ship.

Holding on to the bow railing and gazing out upon the expanse of ocean before us, his countenance became noticeably more serious. And after a prolonged, reflective pause, he turned to me and in a low, somewhat cautious tone of voice, began to speak:

"Last night, Dr. Laughton, I had a truly amazing dream. Queen Isabella… the legendary Catholic Monarch… was standing before me. She was radiant and beautiful beyond words. She gazed at me and said; *'I know what is in your heart. You are ready now. Ask Dr. Laughton to teach you the way of prayer he learned in the desert.'*

That was all she said, Doc… and then I woke up. It was an unusually powerful dream. And so I humbly ask you; did you learn something new in the desert? If so, could you please teach me?"

"Yes, Captain Raul, I did learn a new way of prayer and I would be happy to teach you. Why don't we meet tomorrow evening after dinner on the private deck outside your office. The sun will be setting and the day will be 'breathing cool;' it should be lovely."

Up until this point, Stuart and I had been assuming the captain knew *La Imagen Viva* was on board and had been directed to keep it a secret. Now, however, it was clear he had no knowledge of the historic contents of that mysterious crate stored in the room for special cargo. This led us to believe the crew members Stuart overheard had opened the crate without permission to see what valuable item it contained; perhaps with the intention of stealing it.

The Masters of Interior Space were overjoyed to hear of the missionary activity of Queen Isabella, even before it was officially determined she would be beatified. But, amazingly, it got better! It turned out that within the next twenty four hours, nine sailors came to me and reported having had the same dream.

Stuart told me that, of the nine crew members who wanted to learn the way of prayer suggested to them by the Queen, three were the very individuals he had overheard speaking about how *La Imagen Viva* was onboard the ship. It would appear, then, that those three sailors had come to know the presence of *La Imagen Viva* by accident... perhaps the crate opened as they were moving it... and not by any corrupt intention.

Otherwise, realizing they were not living a virtuous life and therefore lacked the foundation necessary to support the gift of quiet prayer, our candidate for beatification would have passed them over for sailors who were spiritually ready.

On the evening specified, following dinner, Charlie, Toby, Scoot, and myself, gathered on the captain's private deck and, for the first time, shared The Prayer of Jesus Crucified with people outside of our team... in the middle of the vast, North Atlantic Ocean!

The very next day, Scooter was relaxing in his room when there was a knock on his door. He opened the door and standing there was a young, female sailor holding an envelope in her hand:

"You have mail, monsieur," she said, with a french accent, as she handed him the letter. She then turned and calmly walked away.

Stuart was too stunned to say anything; how could anyone receive mail on a ship in the middle of the ocean? He closed the door and immediately looked at the envelope. The only thing on the face of the envelope was his name; no stamp or postal marking of any kind.

He imagined the letter was probably from a member of the ship's crew; perhaps someone who attended the workshop. But the ship did have its own stationary and, chances are, a crew member would have used it. At this point, Stuart's curiosity was fully engaged. He sat down and opened the letter:

To whom it may concern:

Stuart McKenzie, Charlotte Mahfoudh, Tobias Trisong, and Dr. James Laughton are my servants. I have sent them to Manhattan, New York City, on a special mission.

Please do not obstruct them in any way. If possible, please help and facilitate their work as they carry out this important mission. Know that I am with them and I will bless anyone who offers them assistance.

Sincerely,

+ The Eternal, Living God, Creator and Father of All +

If Stuart was stunned when he received the letter, he was rendered practically speechless when he read it. A letter from... GOD? Was such a thing even possible? Well, actually, he thought, hadn't we received a mission from God? Then why not a letter? He folded the letter and stuffed it in his pants' back pocket for future reference.

CHAPTER SIXTEEN

On the morning of the tenth day at sea, just as we were finishing our breakfast, one of the sailors told us the captain wanted to meet with all of us in his office:

"In about half an hour we will be entering New York Harbor, the best natural harbor in the world," said the captain, "and there are some things we need to discuss regarding your disembarkment. You may remember how, when you told me earlier that your mission was in Manhattan, I shared with you the new policy that only cruise ships and other tourist vessels are permitted to dock at Manhattan.

"So we will be docking at the Brooklyn Piers, which is part of Long Island and on the other side of the East River from Manhattan. To get to Manhattan, you will have to cross the river by way of the Brooklyn Bridge. The dockmaster where we will be pulling in is a very good friend of mine and has already agreed to 'look the other way' when you disembark.

"From that point on, you are on your own. You will have to make your way to the entrance of the *Brooklyn Bridge Pedestrian Walkway,* where Tillary Street and Boerum Place intersect. Once you arrive on the other side of the bridge, you will be in Lower Manhattan.

"From there, you can head uptown to Little Italy, Chinatown, Soho, the Bowery, Greenwich Village, Gramercy Park, Chelsea, the Garment District, Broadway, Carnegie Hall, Times Square, NASDAQ World Headquarters, the Empire State Building, Madison Square Garden, Rockefeller Center, Central Park, Fifth Avenue, St. Patrick's Cathedral, the Waldorf Astoria… just to name a few places uptown you may want to visit.

"Or, you could head downtown to Wall Street, the Financial District, the New York Stock Exchange, Federal Hall, Tribeca, and the World Trade Center. Stuart… has the Spirit given you any more specific guidance regarding your Manhattan mission?"

"Yes," replied Stuart, "we will be heading downtown to the New York Stock Exchange, on the corner of Broad and Wall Street, directly across from Federal Hall and the famous statue of George Washington."

"Federal Hall," I added (ever the historian), "is the place where George Washington, the first President of the United States, was sworn in."

"Benjamin Lake," continued Stuart, "a dynamic Catholic and longtime resident of Manhattan, will be meeting us there. The Exchange… or, *The Big Board*, as it is sometimes called… has been closed to the public since 9/11. But Benjamin has clearance and he will get us on to the trading floor."

"Well… good luck with that," said Captain Raul, "looking like Arabs, and all. You know… the camels, the beards, the long hair, the Berber robes, the headgear; well, you sort of... stand out!"

"We will be fine," replied Stuart, "from what I've heard, being outstanding is what New York City is all about!"

"In that case," offered Toby with a smile, "we will fit right in!"

"Exactly!" said Charlie, in concurrence.

Our caravan disembarked the *Rocinante* without a hitch, and we headed in the direction of the Brooklyn Bridge, using the smaller, rarely used roads close to the river. We were only around half a mile away from where we had docked when we came upon some young people sitting on the grass in a little park. The site was on a pier that was a recreation area and was called... Brooklyn Bridge Park/Pier 2 Field & Roller Rink.

When they spotted us, the three teenagers became greatly excited, jumped up and ran over to meet us:

"WOW! You guys and your camels are total dope!" said the young man who appeared to be the leader of this little group of teens, "Are you with the circus? I know the circus is at Madison Square Garden this week."

"No... we are not with the circus. We are Masters of Interior Space, and we have been sent here by God. Our mission is in Manhattan, and we are on our way to the Brooklyn Bridge so we can cross the river."

"YO! slow down, dude. Masters of...WHAT? Is that a new Brooklyn gang?" asked the teen, "Because we're the Latin

Kings. That's why we're wearing black and gold; those are our gang colors. Do you guys have colors, or any other identifiers?"

"The only identifier we have is this one hanging around our neck," replied Scooter, as he pointed to his crucifix, "Jesus crucified."

"Cool... I like it!" said the young gang member, "Real gangsta stuff right there... powerful dope, homie... powerful."

"Thanks, friend," replied Scooter, with a smile, "I'm glad you like it."

"I'm Jorge, but everyone calls me Tigre. This is my posse: the girl is Esmeralda; and, technically, she's a Latin Queen. The other boy is Mateo; we call him Lobo (Wolf). Yo, master dude, I really like that creature on the back of the   burro... totally rad! He looks like a mini-Yoda... with fur!"

"Would it be ok if I went over and pet him?" asked Esmeralda, "He's so cute; he looks like a puppy. What's his name?"

"His name is Alypius;" replied Scooter, "he's a baby fox... a kit... and he's very friendly. Yes, Esmeralda... you can pet him.

"But to answer your question, Tigre, we are not a street gang; we're missionary disciples of our Lord, Jesus. My name is Scooter. But it is a pleasure to meet you, Esmeralda, and Lobo. Thank you for introducing yourselves. You are the first people we have met here in New York City."

"Hey, just a heads up," said Tigre, "You're not going to be able to cross on the Brooklyn Bridge. The Pedestrian Walkway is closed today for repairs."

Stuart closed his eyes, bowed his head, and paused in silence for about a minute:

"Scooter… you ok?" asked Tigre, "Speak to me dude! Sorry to drop a bomb on you about the bridge. What are you doing?"

"Excuse me, Tigre," said Stuart, "I was listening to the Spirit to get some direction."

"Listening to the Spirit?" replied Tigre, "Did he say anything?"

"Yes… he did," answered Stuart.

"Well… what did he say?" asked Tigre, in a frustrated tone.

"He told me we should walk across the river," replied Stuart, calmly.

"Walk across the river? With the camels, the burro, the fox… and your whole posse?" asked Tigre, in amazement.

"Yes," replied Scooter.

"Hey, listen up, Scooter," said Tigre, "that spirit you're listening to… does he hate you? You take one step in that river and you're history! You feel me, Bro… Gone! You'll sink like a stone."

"We'll be fine, Tigre; where is your faith?" replied Stuart, "Can you show us a place on this pier where we can have access to the water?"

"Yeah, follow me," replied Tigre, "There's a ramp that leads down to a floating dock where people can launch their kayaks."

CHAPTER SEVENTEEN

When all of us were finally gathered together on the floating dock and preparing the caravan for its momentous journey across the river, Tigre said:

"Look… I can see that you guys are dead serious. You really are going to step off this dock and into the river, aren't you?"

"*Onto* the river, Tigre," replied Scooter.

"I'll call 911 as soon as you sink into the water," said Tigre, as he took his phone out of his backpack.

"You can put your phone back in your pack, Tigre; you won't be needing it," replied a perfectly calm and confident Scooter, "I see a pier across the way; is that the pier that serves Wall Street?"

"Yes; that's Pier 11," replied Tigre, "Wall Street? Is that where you're going?"

"Yes," said Stuart, "the New York Stock Exchange will be our first stop."

"OK," said Tigre, "Wall Street is directly across from the pier. Just pass under the FDR Drive and you'll see it."

"Tigre," asked Stuart, "you are from here; what do you think the reaction would be of anyone who sees our caravan walking on the water?"

"Considering how, here in The Big Apple," began Tigre, "people have been conditioned by seeing all kinds of unusual and incredible things, my guess would be they would think it was some sort of trick… like a hologram or something. Or, that a film company was shooting a scene for a movie and just below the surface of the water was a submarine of some kind supporting you. I don't think the first 'go to' explanation would be that it was a miracle."

"Wow… that's actually kinda funny, don't you think, Tigre!" replied Scooter.

"Yeah, homie… it's hilarious!" said Tigre with a chuckle, "Anything can happen here in New York City. That's one of the reasons we get so many tourists from all around the world. But, as you mentioned, you guys are not tourists; you're here with a purpose.

"And… strange as it may seem, I'm actually starting to have a sense that God really is with you because, if ever there was the perfect time to lead a camel caravan across this river, right now is that time. There are no ferries in sight; there's no wind, not even a gentle breeze; and the surface of the river is like glass. Also, it's slack water; which means the tide is neither coming in nor going out; so the river is completely still.

"It will stay slack for around thirty minutes. The pier is less than half a mile away, so, although I don't know anything about walking on water, you should make the pier before the tide changes."

"Thank you, Tigre," said Scoot, "you've been a great help. God will bless you!"

"Oh, Scooter," said Tigre, "one final thing: if you and your caravan do make it across this river, me and my posse will leave the Latin Kings and join the Masters."

"Excellent, Tigre!" replied Scooter with enthusiasm, "But you are *already* a Master of Interior Space, you just don't realize it. And you are not alone; this is the main reason we have been sent here. Our mission is to remind people of who they are... their dignity and giftedness.

"Meet us tomorrow at noon in front of the main entrance to the Empire State Building on Fifth Avenue, and bring with you as many leaders of the various gangs as you can. I have a feeling that after they hear you describe what you are about to witness, they will want to meet us. Adios, friends... see you soon!"

Stuart turned toward Charlie and, in his capacity as leader of the mission, said:

"Charlie... use your gift and tell Augustine to lead the caravan out onto the river."

"Augustine," called out Charlie, without hesitation, "step onto the river and lead the caravan to the pier on the opposite side."

Immediately, Augustine stepped off the dock onto the river and began walking as if he was on solid ground. He was followed by Scooter on Miltiades, Charlie on Monica, Toby on

Cyprian, and me on Tertullian. Within seconds, we were already a good distance away from the floating dock, where we left Tigre, Lobo and Esmeralda in a temporary state of suspended animation; with their jaws dropped down onto their chests and a wide-eyed, mesmerized expression plastered on their "frozen" faces.

Witnessing a burro, a fox, and a caravan of camels with riders, walking on water, well… things such as this have their effect; those three *ex*-Latin Kings would never be the same!

The crossing could not have gone any smoother. There was not so much as the tiniest ripple on the water and the camels thought they were walking on sand. As we drew nearer to Pier 11, some people began to gather and take photos. Unhindered, we stepped onto the floating dock, then filed up the ramp and on to the pier itself.

As we paraded down the length of the pier on our way to Wall Street, dock workers and visitors stepped out of our way and stared in amazement:

"You were walking on water!" exclaimed one woman, "How did you do that?"

"Faith," replied Stuart, with consummate serenity.

CHAPTER EIGHTEEN

It was 10 am on a weekday, so the morning rush hour was over and we had no trouble marching up Wall Street in the direction of the NYSE (New York Stock Exchange). Charlie and Toby asked me if we would be passing the iconic *Charging Bull of Wall Street*. I said it was nearby and if we made a slight detour, we could pass it. Scooter agreed to the detour and said seeing it would be good preparation for our visit to the NYSE.

So we changed course a bit and within a few minutes, we were standing directly in front of the giant, lifelike sculpture; which was surrounded by tourists taking selfies and group photos of them hugging and kissing the bull's enormous, bronze head.

After a couple of minutes, the tourists moved on and we had a clear view of the bull. Up until that point, our animals did not know what all the fuss was about. But when they finally were able to make out the complete outline of the sculpture, they flinched and backed away a step. Alypius gave the deepest, most threatening series of growls we had ever heard him make. It was clear they were startled and thought the bull was real and about to charge.

A little girl standing nearby noticed our animals' frightened reaction. Her little heart was touched, and she immediately ran up to the sculpture and slapped the bull on its snout to prove to our caravan it was not a real bull. And it worked! The animals immediately let down their guard and relaxed.

Charlie, for her part, was moved, not by the realistic quality of the sculpture, but by the controversial message it conveyed:

"How ironic that this proud, threatening bull should be facing off with a humble, defenseless burro. A burro carried our holy Mother, pregnant with the Son of God, to a humble stable in Bethlehem. Another burro carried that same Son of God into Jerusalem at the beginning of the Passover festival. And before Jesus entered Jerusalem on that burro, standing atop a hill outside the walls, he wept for the city."

"Yes," added Toby, "and in Eastern tradition, the burro is an animal of peace, and the horse is an animal of war. If a king or a general entered a city on a horse, it was a sign he was planning for war. If he entered on a burro, it meant he was seeking peace. We have come to this city with a message of peace; a message desperately needed here, but one that this ferocious bull simply does not communicate."

"I can't help but reflect," continued Charlie, "on how this Charging Bull is a world famous symbol for the strength and efficacy of capitalism, and yet, as that innocent little girl pointed out, the bull is not real; it's deceptive. So too… capitalism! It purports itself to be the 'savior' of mankind and the definitive cure for global poverty… but this is not true! It is not the solution to all of man's woes… the panacea it is often hailed to be; as proposed by the bold and overconfident demeanor of this sculpture.

Capitalism may be the best system the world has devised thus far, but it is far from perfect. And to this day, its serious flaws have been almost completely… and studiously, I might add… unacknowledged."

When Charlie finished relating her beautiful reflection, a reflection that drew upon her training in philosophy, just as Toby's contribution manifested his work in Peace Studies, I felt compelled to wrap up our encounter with that braggadocious symbol of financial power and dominance by sharing this quote from Christopher Dawson:

"The great fault of modern democracy… a fault that is common to the capitalist and the socialist… is that it accepts economic wealth as the end of society and the standard of personal happiness."

"Having been duly prepared by this providential period of reflection and recollection," declared Stuart, "we are now ready to meet up with Benjamin Lake and our brothers and sisters at the NYSE."

CHAPTER NINETEEN

"Thank you for meeting us here, Benjamin," said Stuart, as he reached down to shake Benjamin Lake's hand.

"Just as the Lord told Ananias to meet with Saul of Tarsus at the home of Judas on Straight Street (Acts 9:11), he told me to meet with you at the NYSE on Wall Street!" replied a delighted Benjamin, "It's a pleasure to finally meet you and your team. Now, if you follow me, I will lead your caravan around back to the service entrance."

Benjamin used his official pass to open the motorized delivery door, and we were met by a security guard who was clearly shocked upon seeing the caravan. I raised my right hand in a gesture of blessing and said: "Peace be with you."

The guard immediately collapsed to the ground and fell into a deep, peaceful slumber. The spiritual description for this type of response is that the person has been "Slain in the Spirit." This was not my conscious intention, but it did facilitate the mission and we continued on to the trading floor.

We entered the room and began to move to a good position from which we could be easily seen and heard. Amazingly enough, you would think that the presence of a burro, a fox, four camels, and four people dressed in Berber robes wearing large crucifixes, would attract some attention; it did not, so absorbed were the traders in their "plotting and scheming."

Not until Stuart turned, pointed to me, and said… "Speak!" did the traders give us their attention. Benjamin handed me a microphone, and as soon as I opened my mouth to speak, all the screens shut down:

"My friends, it is a pleasure to be here with you this morning. We have been sent by God from the heart of the Sahara Desert to deliver a message of love. You work very hard here, day in and day out, suffering and enduring incredible stress. Many of your fellow workers, most of whom were still young, have dropped dead on this floor, in your presence, from sudden, massive heart attacks. And for what? So they could have a bit more 'dust' than others have? Yes… DUST; for, in the final analysis, that's all material wealth really is.

"This type of vain, self-defeating, worldly pursuit is not part of God's plan for you. The problem is not so much what you actually do here; the problem is the *spirit* with which you do it! Your true motivation… what is it? Do you ever consider the impact on the poor that may result from the critical financial decisions you make on a daily basis?

"What about the impact of your work on the environment, or the effect these financial activities are having on your spiritual life? Jesus said it would be easier for a camel to pass through the eye of a needle, than for a rich man to enter the Kingdom of God. Here you see a camel standing before you…

does anyone have a needle? Anyone want to test the theory? Good luck with that!

"The point is, your Father loves you, and he wants what is best for you. We were not created for 'having;' we were created for 'being'… for being in love; in love with God and one another. Your lives are focused on 'having.' But when having becomes the focus, you can never have enough! Therefore, you will never be happy; it's like a curse we bring down upon ourselves. This compulsive materialism not only wounds you, but the consumerism it generates is also devastating the planet… our common home.

"Please, think about these things. You are beloved and destined for so much more than just the calculation of worldly gain. We invite you to join us tomorrow at noon in front of the main entrance to the Empire State building where we will be gathering for a small, outdoor luncheon."

The response was truly amazing. I spoke for no more than five minutes and no one said a word while I was speaking. When I finished speaking, there was complete silence until we processed out of the room and the door closed behind us; at which point, all the screens came back on. Benjamin Lake had this to say:

"I've seen many beautiful things in my life, but what I just saw in there was beyond beautiful; it was transformational. Many of those people will never be the same. By the grace of God, you had the full attention of not just their minds and hearts, but their souls as well!

"Let's move on; I know you want to radiate the Trinity at One World Trade Center, so we can continue to chat while we walk. As you know, up until just a year ago, I owned the biggest private bank in the USA, and I was... and still am... a multi-billionaire. But the Lord transformed my heart and called me to start a special mission project in Chiapas, MX. The full story of my conversion can be found in a new, award winning book titled... *To Whom The Heart Decided to Love.*

"In any case, I know most of the big shots here in the financial district and I have arranged for your animals to stay at the new global headquarters of the Goldman Sachs Investment Banking Firm at 200 West Street. It's very close to the Trade Center.

"My friends there have fixed up and sectioned off a corner in the main storage area of the building and outfitted it with hay and such, so the animals will be safe and comfortable for the night. They even hired a veterinarian to examine them and stay with them until you head uptown in the morning.

"Directly behind the headquarters building, and connected by a very artistic, covered pedestrian walkway nicknamed *Goldman Alley,* is the *Conrad New York Hotel.* The Conrad is a luxury hotel owned by the Goldman Sachs Group, Inc. Each of you will have your own suite with a view of the Hudson River. Also, whatever purchases you make in the hotel... for example, in-room dining... will be covered by the hotel.

"Ok... we are almost there; you can see the One World Trade Center building from here."

CHAPTER TWENTY

We enjoyed a great evening and a peaceful night's rest at the Conrad and were back on the street with our caravan at eight in the morning. Our first planned stop on the way to the Empire State Building was to pray at the African Burial Ground National Monument. We had no sooner arrived when a police cruiser pulled in front of us and ordered us to stop.

Two police officers exited the patrol car and approached the caravan, casting puzzled looks at Alypius as they passed him, perched on his "throne" like royalty. There was an older, experienced officer with a rather serious countenance and a younger officer who was smiling and appeared to be much friendlier. The stern officer walked up to Stuart and Miltiades and said:

"I'm assuming all of you are with the circus?"

"No, officer, we are not with the circus," replied Scooter.

"Well, then, what are you doing walking around the city with these large animals?" asked the officer, "Do you have some sort of permit you can show me?"

"Yes, officer, I do," responded Scoot, as he struggled to reach under his robe for the letter in his back pocket.

"Is it from the mayor's office?" asked the officer.

"No," replied Scoot, "higher."

"The governor?" asked the officer.

"Higher," replied Scoot, calmly.

"Higher?" said the officer, "Who is it from?"

"God," replied Scoot, innocently, and in a perfectly tranquil tone of voice.

"GOD!" yelled the officer, "Now I *know* you're with the circus! You're all probably circus clowns and this is some sort of crazy PR stunt. Give me the permit... let me read it."

"This is unbelievable," said the officer to his assistant, while reading the letter, "Take a look at this, Joey... it's signed by God! These people are real comedians!"

"But Al," replied the rookie officer, "it says that if we help, rather than hinder them, God will bless us. Wouldn't you like to receive a blessing from God?"

"Joey... did you really graduate from the academy?" said Al, "Are you such a complete imbecile that you actually believe this letter was sent by God?"

"But look, Al... God signed it! When was the last time you saw a letter signed by God himself?"

"You really are helpless, Joey," replied Al, "You shouldn't even be walking the streets... you should be in some sort of assisted living setup. I can't believe they gave me a complete moron for a partner. To answer your idiotic question... I have *never* seen a letter signed by God himself! And if I had seen one, I would have known immediately that it was a fraud!"

"How could you know for certain it was a fraud?" replied the rookie, "Do you know what God's signature looks like?"

"I do," replied a priest in a black clerical suit who suddenly appeared on the scene.

"And who might you be?" asked Al, sarcastically.

"I'm Father Charles," replied the priest, with a heavy french accent, "and I'm the guardian of this caravan. If you give me the letter, I can verify the authenticity of the signature."

"You're their representative?" asked Al, "And where are you from?"

"Heaven," was the priest's honest reply.

"You see, Al," said Joey, excitedly, "He's from Heaven! That's proof the letter is real!"

"Excuse my simple friend, here, Father," said Al, "He was dropped on his head as a newborn. I'm Catholic, so I'm familiar with 'Catholic shorthand;' you're from Gate of Heaven parish in Ozone Park. Take a look at this letter and tell my nitwit partner here, who, sorry to say, also happens to be Catholic, the truth."

"Yes... this is his signature," replied Fr. Charles, "I know it well and I'd recognize it anywhere; this is definitely God's signature."

"OK... we're done here!" cried out the exasperated officer, "Between the clown on the camel, Yoda on the donkey, the letter from God, my brain-dead partner, and this French priest from Heaven... if I stay here any longer, I'll be the one in need of an institution!

"Try to stay in the street and avoid walking on the sidewalk. See you at the circus; I'll be bringing my grandchildren. Stay safe."

"God bless you!" replied Fr. Charles, with great sincerity. Then he turned, smiled at us, and walked down the street into a crowd of people and disappeared.

CHAPTER TWENTY-ONE

When we arrived at our next stop, Chinatown, the animals must have been hungry because they led us directly to the street that served as an outdoor produce market. On display on both sides of the street were countless types of fresh vegetables and fruits.

The children of the shop owners spotted the caravan and were overjoyed by the sight. They came running out to greet us and began petting the animals. They asked us if they could feed the animals, and we said it was a splendid idea and would be greatly appreciated.

The parents gave them appropriate items to feed our caravan, and the children had the time of their lives doing so. Everyone was happy; the parents, the children, the Masters, and the animals. Some of the teenagers asked where we were going, and we told them we were on our way to Little Italy, and then to the Empire State Building. Charlie invited them to join our caravan and, with typical youthful exuberance, they responded with a resounding… "YES!"

With around twenty teenagers walking alongside us, looking more like a small parade than a caravan, we entered Little Italy and were just in time for some sort of big hubbub taking place on the sidewalk in front of an old brownstone building.

We dismounted our camels and went over to see what was going on. Apparently, a middle aged Italian man... a well-known and well-loved member of the community... exited his building, descended the stoop to the sidewalk, and instantly fell to the ground, dead.

The people were crying and in shock, and no one seemed to know what to do. Stuart knelt down close to the body and said:

"We are Catholic missionaries. Would you allow us to pray over this poor man?"

The man's friends and relatives, seeing our distinctive garb and the large crucifixes around our necks, must have thought we were members of a religious order and said they would be most grateful for any spiritual assistance we could offer.

Stuart asked the three of us to gather around the body and to place our hands on the man's head and chest. Then he closed his eyes, bowed his head, and in a prayerful, personal manner, began to pray:

"Father... we do not know this man; but you know and love him from all eternity, and you made him for yourself. We ask you to hear our prayer, and the heartfelt prayers of his family and friends. Father... through the intercession of our official heavenly assistants, St. Therese of Lisieux and St. Charles de Foucauld, we beg you, in your everlasting love and mercy... bring this man back to life."

A few seconds passed and we began to feel something; we could sense a pulse and a heartbeat. Color returned to the man's face. His fingers began to move, and his eyeballs, still covered by their closed lids, began twitching. Suddenly, his eyes popped wide open, he sat up straight and said:

"What happened? Why are all of you here? Has there been some kind of accident?"

Needless to say, the people were very rejoiced and extremely grateful. One man in particular, who was the resuscitated man's brother, owned a large Italian delicatessen right on the other side of the street. He asked us to give him a few minutes so he could prepare some food for our journey.

After stuffing the leather saddlebag on Toby's camel with four footlong heros, soda, chips, and Italian cookies, we continued on to the Empire State Building. Our entourage now contained an additional twenty people from Little Italy. What started out as a small caravan was quickly turning into a world class cavalcade, with his royal highness... Alypius of Thagaste... serving as the Grand Marshal!

As we set out on the two-mile trek to the Empire State Building in midtown Manhattan, I could not help but reflect on the loving providence of our heavenly Father. He provided everything we could ever need or want... right down to the Italian cookies! And yet, most people live in a perpetual state of anxiety, conducting their lives as though they were in constant danger of not having sufficient resources to sustain them.

How liberating are the words of Jesus when he says:

"Therefore I tell you, do not be anxious about your life… is not life more than food, and the body more than clothing? Look at the birds of the air. They do not sow or reap or gather into barns… and yet your heavenly Father feeds them. Are you not more valuable than they?

"Seek first the Kingdom of God and his righteousness, and all these things will be added unto you." (Matthew 6:25-26, and, 6:33)

CHAPTER TWENTY-TWO

"Wow! This really is quite a skyscraper, isn't it!" exclaimed Charlie, looking up at the Empire State Building from its base.

"Yes," I replied, "for many years, it was the tallest building in the world, and was rendered a cultural icon and globally memorialized by King Kong's epic, free climb to the top, and subsequent, tragic fall to the street below."

Our ranks had grown substantially on our tedious push uptown. We had picked up at least another fifty people along the way; some traders from the NYSE, a few brokers from Goldman Sachs, some actors and actresses in Soho, some musicians in Greenwich Village, and some homeless people from... who knows where!

Believe it or not, Tigre was waiting for us when we arrived. Accompanying him were not only his posse... Lobo and Esmeralda... but the leaders of eight prominent New York City gangs: The Silenciosos, The Rat Hunters, The Nietas, The Matatones, The Zulu Nation, The Five Prisoners, and The Latin Kings with their allies... The Bloods.

The leader of the Kings, a middle-aged fellow named Pedro, walked up to Stuart and gave him a big hug:

"It's an honor to meet you, Scooter; my people told me all about you, your posse, and your mission." said Pedro, "We are here to help. We saw the pictures on the news of your caravan walking on the water. Dude, that was the ultimate dope! You have earned our respect, and that's why all these gang leaders are here. Tell us how we can be of assistance."

"Thank you, Pedro," said Scooter, "tiene hambre... Pedro?" (are you hungry?) asked Scooter, "Si... seguro, hermano; ¡tengo mucho hambre!" (Yes, for sure, brother; I'm very hungry!)"

"Perfect," replied Scooter, "Everyone here is starved from the long hike uptown, so let's have some lunch. Toby, please pray over the food in your saddlebag and distribute it to the crowd."

"Toby walked over to Cyprian, his camel, and placing his two hands on the saddlebag containing the donated food from the Italian delicatessen, said the following prayer:

"Father in Heaven, we, your children, are hungry. Therefore, with childlike confidence in your loving providence, I ask you... *Give us this day, our daily bread!*"

Then he opened the saddlebag and began distributing the food to a famished group of around one hundred people. As quickly as he withdrew food from the bag, it was miraculously replenished. After fifteen minutes, when everyone present was enjoying a delicious Italian hero, along with a soda, chips, and cookies, the saddlebag still contained the original amount of food.

Pedro walked over to Cyprian, looked in the bag, turned to Toby and, with a look of astonishment on his face, said:

"How did you do that? What kind of powers are you guys tapping into? You're like the illusionists in the movie… *Now You See Me*. This is wild! You guys need to be *real* careful; with this kind of power, you're gonna have the CIA on your tail. We don't have anything close to your abilities, and the FBI is all over us."

"The good things we do, Pedro," replied Toby, "are the work of God; we do not have any special powers. We are not like the Avengers, or the X-Men, whose powers are rooted in the individual and are merely exaggerated expressions of the physical forces already present in the material world. We are useless servants who can do nothing, and the genesis of all our works is spiritual.

"This loving humility leads us into an intimate communion with God… which gives birth to the wonders you have been witnessing. But as to your astute observation, it would not surprise me if the CIA were to take a 'professional' interest in our mission… not so much because of the marvels themselves, but because of our message; Jesus was well known for his tendency to… *rock the boat!*"

Needless to say, Pedro was even more fascinated by the captivating explanation given him by Toby. When everyone was finished eating, Stuart mounted his camel and moved to a strategic position where his voice could be heard by all:

"My friends, God is with us. You just witnessed the greatness of his love for you. I invite you to continue walking with us. The next stop will be our last and the most important. It will be the culmination of our special mission here in Manhattan.

"We will be heading crosstown to the United Nations Headquarters where the Masters of Interior Space will address the General Assembly. In case you are wondering, our visit is not on their agenda... but it is on God's, and that's all that matters."

"If you are not on the agenda," asked one of the traders from the NYSE, "How do you plan to get into the building? There's tons of security!"

"Many people are not aware of this," began Stuart, "but the United Nations Headquarters, while it is located in New York City, is not actually under the jurisdiction of the city. Nor is it under the jurisdiction of the US Federal Government. The land occupied by the Headquarters is under the sole administration of the United Nations and is technically *extraterritorial* by virtue of a treaty agreement with the US government.

"But what you will witness today is that, ultimately, the UN is under the jurisdiction of God. We will get into the General Assembly, and we will speak; you can count on it. As to 'how' this will be accomplished... I have no idea. The Spirit will direct us on site. Therefore, we must remain completely open to his direction.

"Are you up for a beautiful, spiritual adventure?"

"Si... VAMONOS!" yelled Pedro excitedly, with his hand raised and pointing in the direction of the UN.

CHAPTER TWENTY-THREE

As we marched crosstown, we gained another fifty people, and our cavalcade morphed into an outright parade. At one point, Pedro, who along with the other gang leaders was serving as a security vanguard, approached Scooter and, pointing to a drone hovering above them, said:

"You see that? I told you 'big brother' would be watching you. You want me to take it out? I'd be happy to bust a cap in that thing's punk ass."

"Pedro," asked Scooter, "Are you armed?"

"Am I armed?" replied Pedro, excitedly, "Is the Pope Catholic? Of course, I have a gat with me! All of us gang leaders are strapped. For us to come out like this in the open is super dangerous. Each of us has deadly enemies in rival gangs, who, given the right opportunity, would love to waste us."

"OK… understood, Pedro," said Scooter, "but regarding this drone, let's just let it be. This mission is too important to put at risk by unnecessarily antagonizing anyone."

"You're right, Jefe," replied Pedro, "We'll just leave it alone."

"OK, so here's what you are going to do when we get there," announced Stuart when we were five blocks away from the UN, "You will do nothing. The less you do, the more He can do. You will not protest, you will not demonstrate; you will simply be a quiet, peaceful presence and a holy witness to the dignity, giftedness, and high calling of man.

"You will take your cues from the prophet Isaiah, who, when describing the coming Messiah, said: 'I will put my Spirit on him, and he will bring justice to the nations. He will not shout or cry out, or raise his voice in the streets.' (Isaiah 42:1-2)

"If anyone asks you why you are there, tell them you are radiating the Holy Trinity to the United Nations General Assembly. If you are questioned by the media, you can tell them you are there to support your friends who are addressing the General Assembly. If they ask who your friends are, just say they are Masters of Interior Space sent by God from the heart of the Sahara desert.

"Chances are, they will not understand any of this and will want to see for themselves what's going on in the General Assembly... and this is perfect! We need them to be there so our message will go out to the whole world."

When we were one block from the UN, a police car pulled up to the front of the parade and the officer told Pedro there was no problem, but he did need to speak with Scooter. The officer was Al... the same officer the group encountered earlier at the African Burial Ground National Monument.

Scooter walked over to the patrol car and Al, donning a big smile, asked him to come and sit in the front seat so they could have a private conversation:

"This morning when I came across you and your friends, I didn't believe a word you said. I didn't know what to make of you. I was on my way to the hospital to visit my daughter and I was in a hurry; that's why I decided to leave you to your own devices.

"My daughter, who has three children in middle school, has been in a vegetative state for the past week due to a brain aneurysm. Just before I came upon your caravan, her physician called me to say she was at death's door and probably would not survive into the afternoon.

"When I arrived at her hospital room, my daughter was sitting up, fully conscious, and eating scrambled eggs! She was surrounded by nurses, doctors, and various family members, and everyone was happy and smiling. Her physician said that 20 minutes before I arrived, she had a truly miraculous recovery. He said he had never seen anything like it before.

"Right then, I remembered what your letter said about how God would bless anyone who facilitated your mission. And suddenly it all clicked; my daughter was healed the instant the French priest from Heaven said… 'God bless you!'

"And so I am here to apologize and to ask if there is anything I can do for you. Where are you heading now?"

"Well," replied Stuart, "perhaps there is something you can do to help. God wants us to address the United Nations General Assembly (UNGA) today, but we are not on the agenda and, with all the security, we are not sure how we will gain entry."

"And I thought today was *my* lucky day," said Al, "but after you hear what I am about to say, you will realize it's your lucky day as well. Stuart… my younger brother, Kyle, is the director of the entire security program at the United Nations! He already knows how my daughter's miraculous healing came about, so I'm positive he will help you get in. Let me give him a call right now."

Al spoke with his brother, Kyle, and they came up with a solid plan. Al would take Scooter, Charlie, Doc, Toby, and Alypius, around back to a secret, subterranean entrance where there is no security, and Kyle would make sure the door was unlocked.

"When you get inside," directed Al, "go up the stairs and follow the signs to the Assembly Hall. Enter the hall, go straight to the rostrum, and begin to speak as though you were actually on the agenda. Kyle will make sure the President of the Assembly's microphone is neutralized by technical problems.

"You will have around five minutes before anyone realizes something unofficial is taking place. After your five minutes are up, leave the rostrum and quickly make your way to the nearest exit that leads out to the street. Once on the street, you will be safe; UN security only has jurisdiction on UN property."

CHAPTER TWENTY-FOUR

"Distinguished UN Representatives," began Stuart, leaning into the podium microphone, "it's an honor to be here with you today, and to have this opportunity to share some thoughts about a very serious topic; the state of Man in the Third Millennium. Notice I said 'Man,' and not the world.

"My name is Scooter. To my left are Charlie and Toby. And to my right is Doc. Sitting In front of me on the podium is Alypius, our well-behaved, Fennec Fox kit. We are Masters of Interior Space, and we have traveled all the way from the Sahara Desert because God wanted us to visit with you.

"As I'm sure all of you are aware, the world is experiencing a historic period of civilizational crisis as it moves tumultuously into a new era of globalization. There are a number of different ideas in play regarding the best way to facilitate this momentous paradigm shift.

"All of these ideas have more to do with the material world around us than with Man, per se. For example, climate change is a big concern. So big that a state of global panic seems to be taking shape on the horizon. Health, Communications, Energy, Technology (AI), economic development, the question of the continuance of sovereign nation states, the colonization of outer space… these are some of the other major concerns people have been focusing on.

"Exasperating this stressful situation is the fact that, amidst this great, chaotic charge into the future, Man is being dangerously objectified. He is being treated as just one of the many parts in this new puzzle, when in truth, Man is the key… the cornerstone. And if, at this critical turning point, we don't get our understanding of 'Man' right… we can forget about the puzzle. This is not to say that Man does not participate in objective reality; or worse… that there is no objective reality.

"We are simply saying that the understanding of Man has not just been completely skewed in favor of objectification, but that now, it is taken for granted that the interior life does not exist, and in fact, never has existed.

"The objectification of Man is, unfortunately, something that has been happening since the beginning of recorded history. But at this present moment in time, this gross distortion has grown to such a terrifying degree that previous levels of objectification now appear relatively benign.

"The point is that the time has come to recognize and fully embrace the unique giftedness of Man… a special being with a profound interior life. At this unprecedented crossroads in history, we have the opportunity to correct this long standing blindspot regarding the truth about Man.

"If we continue to ignore this truth regarding the interiority of Man, there is no way we will ever be able to deal effectively with the future that awaits us. The reason for this is two-fold: all of the serious problems we are now facing are a result of having repressed for so long this fundamental truth about Man. Many years ago, the renowned Austrian Psychiatrist, Viktor Frankl, began to approach and open up this subject... albeit, from a psychological perspective... in his book *The Unconscious God* (1943).

"But the deeper issue is not so much a question of consciousness as it is a question of spiritual life, expressed in the interior relationship a person has with the living God; a relationship initiated by God. When people commit themselves to this interior relationship with the God who is love, they will be gifted with the wisdom and strength to resolve and deal effectively with whatever problems they encounter in the world around them.

"This is why, at the very beginning of this humble presentation, I spoke of... 'the state of Man;' as opposed to... 'the state of the world.' The reason for this is that the state of the world is dependent upon the state of Man. And this is precisely what, for two millennia, we have been overlooking.

"The situation brings to mind the classic example of the person who has been running around the house, frantically searching for their hat, until they look in the mirror and discover that the hat has been on their head the whole time!"

At this particular point in Stuart's presentation, an exceedingly marvelous, supernatural event was set in motion. The four of us began to rise off the rostrum. When it first started, we were elevated an inch or two off the floor. But it continued until we were floating in midair, two feet above the podium! Alypius had "lift-off" as well!

For some reason unknown to us, we had been granted the gift of levitation. Talk about stage presence... the Lord certainly knows how to "elevate" a performance he himself is invested in! The amazing thing, however, was that we were completely unruffled by the fact that we were suddenly suspended in midair, six feet off the ground. And Stuart just continued speaking without missing a beat, as if nothing unusual was occurring.

The same cannot be said about the audience. They were paralyzed with astonishment and just sat there motionless, staring at us and trying to figure out exactly what it was they were witnessing. And I guess that was the whole point. There really is no "figuring it out," but everyone certainly got the "memo" loud and clear; God was revealing his presence in his servants, and showing his approval of their message.

"By the way," continued Stuart calmly, from his in-flight location, "you may have noticed that the little contingent in front of you is floating in midair. I just want to assure you... this is not some kind of a trick; we had nothing to do with it. We did not plan it nor did we have any advance notice that this was going to take place. But we can say from experience that this is how God works... He's full of surprises!

"And so, my friends, I would ask you to look in the mirror and see that the hat you have been searching for is where it has been all along; right on top of your head! Our situation is not quite as desperate as most people would have us believe; there really is an answer to the future of Man. It's just that we have been looking in all the wrong places. Now is the time to finally look in the right place."

This was the point in the speech when Stuart and company began to slowly descend to their original positions at the rostrum.

"And let's be clear... the moon isn't the right place; Mars isn't the right place. The right place isn't anywhere 'out there'... external to Man. The answers lie within Man. The only world we desperately need to discover is waiting there within us. It has always been there, but we were much too busy playing around with 'solutions' that very often gave birth to new problems. And often enough, those new problems were worse than the original ones we were trying to resolve.

"Now is the time to end the dysfunctional and self-defeating habit we have been clinging to for centuries, and which Jesus described so well when he said... *Blind guides! You strain out the gnat, and swallow a camel!* (Matthew 23:24).

"Also, it is not uncommon to discover that, with infused wisdom... a gift associated with the interior life... what we originally labeled a problem, is not a problem at all but only a false perception caused by misguided, and uninspired thinking.

"And so my friends, to conclude, we call ourselves Masters of Interior Space because we believe this is what each and every human person was created to be; a master of the inner life of prayer and communion with God. This is, and always has been, Man's greatest gift; and it defines us as human persons.

"If we enter into this truth, there will be no need for existential dread or angst of any kind regarding the future because we will know that the transcendent peace in the depth of our souls *is* the future. As St. Augustine said so well in his Confessions... *Our hearts are restless until they rest in you.*"

Stuart paused for a moment at this point to check his watch, and then said:

"OOPS! Time to go. It's been real... Adios!"

And with that, the masters quickly left the Hall, rushed to the nearest exit, and proceeded out to the safety of the street.

CHAPTER TWENTY-FIVE

A few days later, we were back at my farmhouse in Indiana:

"Wow, Doc," exclaimed Charlie, as we pulled into my property, "Your land is really beautiful! The grassy hills, the stream, and the lovely groupings of oak and walnut trees... what a great place for renewal and recollection! And I'm sure the four-legged members of our team will be very happy here as well."

"Yes Doc," said Toby, "This place is awesome!"

"I'm glad you like it," I replied, "All of you are welcome to stay here as long as you like; the house is way too big for just one person. My room is downstairs, but you can take over the second and third floor. Let's go into the house."

We entered the house, and I told the students to go upstairs and decide which room each would take. I had an arrangement with a friendly neighbor who agreed to bring my mail into the house when I was out of town and leave it on the fireplace mantle. So I went into the living room to check my mail:

"Stuart," I yelled, "Could you please come down here for a moment... I'm in the living room."

"Here I am Doc," said Stuart, as he entered the room, "What do you need?"

"Stuart," I said, in a serious tone, "take a good look at the wooden crate in front of the fireplace. Does it look familiar to you?"

"Doc," replied Stuart, as he turned toward me with a mesmerized look on his face, "that's... that's the same shipping crate *La Imagen Viva* was in!"

"That's exactly what I thought, Scoot, based on the description you gave me." I said.

"But Doc," asked Scooter, "if this is *La Imagen Viva*, what is she doing in your living room?"

"I have no idea, Stuart," I replied, "but maybe whoever was protecting the artifact decided that, since the Queen is close to being beatified and since my sincere, lifelong interest in the statue is well known in Spain, it was time for *me* to take care of it."

"I'm speechless, Doc; I'm so excited right now, I really don't know what to say. But everything *you* just said makes sense to me."

"Do you think we should open it right now, Scoot," I said, "to see if it is her?"

"Oh, it's her, Doc," replied Stuart, "I can feel it in my soul. I'm having the same feelings now that I had when I was alone in the vault with her majesty. It's her, Doc... no question about it!"

"OK, I trust your senses in this matter, Stuart, which is why I called on your help. Let's get Charlie and Toby down here so they can meet the person whose mission we just fulfilled."

"Of course, you realize, Doc," began Scooter, "she may not be in her luminescent, conversational mode. Remember… she was out of the crate when she spoke with me; and I was alone. Which, based on the fact that she locked you out of the vault, seemed to be the way she wanted it."

"Good point, Stuart, you are right," I said, "Nevertheless, this is so important, we really need to know if this crate contains *La Imagen Viva*. Please… go upstairs and retrieve the others. When they get here, we'll open the crate together. This could turn out to be a very significant experience for our team, and one of the most memorable moments of our lives."

After explaining the situation to Toby and Charlie, we carefully opened the crate. And sure enough, there she was… *La Imagen Viva*!

"What do you think, Stuart," I said, "You're the only one who has ever seen her before."

"Just as Fr. Foucauld confirmed God's signature," replied Stuart, "I can confirm that this is indeed *La Imagen Viva*."

We stood there in awe for a minute or two and just stared at the beautiful Queen mysteriously present before us.

"What will you do with her, Doc," asked Charlie.

"I don't know," I replied, "This is quite a complicated situation we have here. Some people would say the statue belongs to Spain. But Spain has never admitted the actual existence of the statue. The present government treats the whole question as nothing more than folklore… a medieval legend."

"And the Church?" asked Stuart.

"The Church is even more incredulous!" I said, "The Church shies away from medieval stories about talking statues."

"Maybe she came here because she wants to be a member of our team!" proposed Toby.

We turned and faced one another in an attempt to process this suggestion as a team. Suddenly, Stuart, wearing a big smile, said:

"Well, if she's going to be part of our team, I think we all know what that would entail."

Laughing, the four of us answered in unison:

"She will have to study at Notre Dame!"

The End

Made in the USA
Middletown, DE
29 January 2023

23362946R00086